Somewhere
around the corner

Although we attempt to carefully select all of the books contained in our library, it is not possible to be familiar with every book and the contents before those books are placed on the shelves.

There may also be values presented within some books that are questionable. We would encourage parents to be aware of the books their children are reading and to discuss those books with them.

It is not our intention to remove all controversial resources from our library. All materials will not necessarily present Biblical values. Our aim for students is to develop perception and an ability to be discriminating

Somewhere around the corner

Angus&Robertson
An imprint of HarperCollins*Publishers*

*This book is dedicated to the many people who are (almost) in it:
to my parents, Val French and Barrie Ffrench, and to my son
Edward, who all, in very different ways, work for what they believe
in; to Bryan Sullivan (always); to Geoff Pryor and Val Plumwood,
and everyone else who makes a stand ...
... and, of course, to Gully Jack.*

*The author gratefully acknowledges the assistance of the
Literature Board of the Australia Council.*

Angus&Robertson
An imprint of HarperCollins*Publishers*, Australia

First published in Australia in 1994
Reprinted in 1994, 1995 (twice), 1996 (twice), 1998, 1999
by HarperCollins*Publishers* Pty Limited
ACN 009 913 517
A member of the HarperCollins*Publishers* (Australia) Pty Limited Group
http://www.harpercollins.com.au

HarperCollins*Publishers*
25 Ryde Road, Pymble, Sydney, NSW 2073, Australia
31 View Road, Glenfield, Auckland 10, New Zealand
77-85 Fulham Palace Road, London W6 8JB, United Kingdom
Hazelton Lanes, 55 Avenue Road, Suite 2900, Toronto, Ontario M5R 3L2
and 1995 Markham Road, Scarborough, Ontario M1B 5M8, Canada
10 East 53rd Street, New York NY 10032, USA

National Library of Australia Cataloguing-in-Publication data:

French, Jacqueline.
Somewhere around the corner.
ISBN 0 207 18359 7.
I. Title.
A823.3

Cover: colour photograph by Amanda Smith. Background photographs from a
private collection and the collections of the State Library of New South Wales.
Cover design by Melanie Feddersen
Printed in Australia by Griffin Press Pty Ltd on 79gsm Bulky Paperback

12 11 10 9 8   99 00 01 02

BARBARA

It was hot. The crowd smelt of bitumen, excitement, apprehension. A policeman out the front shouted. Barbara tried to hear, but the policeman's voice was lost in the sway of chants and swing of feet.

She'd been hungry earlier, a tight knot in her belly; but hunger was forgotten now. She'd been confused, but that was gone as well. It was as though all her life until now had disappeared. All that was left was loneliness and fear.

The policeman shouted again. He had a megaphone. Barbara could just glimpse it through the shoulders and the placards up ahead. Was he telling the demonstrators to go away?

The police were moving forward into the crowd, solid-shouldered and purposeful. Someone screamed, then the sound was broken off. The noise of the demonstration changed abruptly. The chants and chatter were gone. It was as though the crowd had one voice now, a high-pitched desperate chatter; one smell, the smell of panic.

Barbara turned frantically. Where were the others? They'd brought her here. They'd tell her what to do. Somehow, somewhere, there must be a corner of the world where she'd be safe. But they were gone, part of the shifting feet, the nameless faces all around.

'Are you all right?'

The old man wore a suit, drab among the tattered clothes around him. He was tall, but leant heavily on a walking stick. He put the other hand on her shoulder. His wrinkles were like the rays of the sun. Barbara stared up at him.

'You scared?'

Barbara nodded.

'Me too. Times like this are always frightening. But you've got to make a stand sometimes. You've got to stand up for what you believe in, even if you're frightened. You've got to believe that you can make things better ...' He broke off with a smile. 'I'm making a speech again. Who are you with? You're not here by yourself?'

'My friends.' She'd only met them yesterday. Like her, they had no place to stay. They had said that she could stick with them, they'd show her how to manage. Was that enough to call them friends? Barbara looked around, desperate.

'They were here a minute ago, but they went over to see someone they knew and—'

'Hey, you'll be right, love. They'll be back.'

'But what do you do,' she broke in, 'when the police come?'

What if they arrested her? Would they put her in gaol, or in a children's home? Would they send her back ...

She couldn't go back. She couldn't.

The man's eyes were old and blue and friendly. 'I'll tell you a secret. A real secret. A girl told it to me years ago. A nice girl, one of the best I've ever known. She was a bit like you. She told me she'd been scared, just the way you are. She said that when you're scared you just go around the corner.'

Someone screamed again. A man shouted, then broke off. The crowd was milling around, confused; some people leaving, some prepared to make a stand. Barbara tried to speak. A shoulder jostled her. She almost fell, but the old man's arm kept her steady. He winced, as though the shock hurt him. 'Around the corner?'

'That's it. You've got to be scared enough to make it happen. I reckon that's why it's never worked for me.'

'But how does it work?' She had to shout to be heard.

'You just imagine.' The old voice was comforting in her ear, as though he was remembering happier times, people that he loved. 'Just shut your eyes and picture yourself walking around a corner. That's what she told me. Somewhere around the corner the world is better. Somewhere around the corner you'll be safe.'

Safety, that's what she wanted. Safety and a home. But how ...

'I don't understand. That girl you knew. Did she walk around the corner? How?'

The old man was staring at her now, properly, as though he'd come back from somewhere far away. He was looking at her hair — she knew it needed washing — and her grubby T-shirt, the jeans stained at the knee, the sweat-shirt she'd grabbed and tied around her waist as she left what had been home. He was going to ask questions. His eyes were kind, but she couldn't cope with questions.

The crowd was shifting, ebbing, flowing. The police were forging through the sea of bodies. A voice screamed high above the crowd, too piercing to tell if it was male or female. It sounded as if the world was screaming. The legs, the arms, the bodies moved. The old man's arm was torn from her shoulder. Suddenly, he was gone. Bodies buffeted her from every side. She couldn't see what was happening. There were people running, but there was no room to run; stumbling, but there was no ground free of feet; crying, but who would hear in all this noise.

The bodies parted suddenly. She could see a policeman hauling a girl off by her hair. The girl was shrieking. Her face was a mouth and frightened eyes. There were more police, and more. The blue of their uniforms filled the world. One was coming towards her. Everyone was gone but her; they'd all moved back. He was looking straight at her. She had to run as well, but her legs were frozen in place — unable to move.

The policeman lifted up his arm.

NO!

But there was no sound, her terror made no noise. Her legs were thick, her arms were weak ... she couldn't speak, she couldn't move ... everything safe and happy was so far away; untouchable, unreachable. There was nowhere in the world to go ...

'Just walk around the corner.' Suddenly, the old man's voice was clear in her mind. Around the corner would be different. Around the corner would be safe. Away from bodies, screams and terror, away from the despair that had been home ...

Her thoughts went blank. Suddenly she could almost see it, a corner somewhere in the distance, clear and solid like it had always been there; it had simply needed terror to clear a pathway in her mind.

The horror of the world around her stilled. She began to move toward the corner slowly, but the air was jelly, almost too thick to take a step. Her legs could move, or did she simply think they moved? One step, two steps. All she had to do was make it around the corner on the edges of her mind ...

For a moment there was silence, then the world was ripped away. She could feel reality tearing like a scrap of paper. She could feel shapes part and merge and melt. The world was spinning on its axis, but she was standing still, caught in a whirlpool that was time and space running free. Her body tumbled with it, the corner in her mind the only thing keeping her safe. She had to walk, she had to move, she had to get around the corner ... one more step, and another.

Someone was helping her. Hands were stretching out. Lots of hands. They were reaching around the corner. They were pulling her, directing her ... suddenly she slid around the corner to the other side.

She tried to focus. This would be the world she'd been promised, this would be security ... but even here the world was molten, a slow deliberate whirling, there was still no firm reality that she could grab. She could feel it tearing at her, but its grasp was different now, ebbing as the whirlpool eased. Gradually the chaos slowed. She was drifting on its edges. There'd be safety here. A few more steps and she'd be free.

Suddenly, there was silence. Birds were singing somewhere, music, there was wind among the trees. The peace seeped into her skin. One more step and she'd be there, among the trees and birds and peace.

It was so hard to move. If she'd been faster perhaps she would have made it, but the peaceful place was gone. The screams were in her ears again, the smells of the crowd and the fear. But these were different. The world was opening up again. Barbara opened her eyes too.

The policeman was still towering over her. His face was hard, a face that did its duty, that shut out everything, except what it had been told to do. But it wasn't him, it wasn't the policeman who'd been there before. It was a different face, a different man, a different uniform.

Barbara blinked, frantic. Maybe if she shut her eyes reality would creep back to what it had been before ... even the smells and voices were strange. There was pavement beneath her feet, not bitumen; buildings, strange buildings. Someone was groaning next to her, blood across his face. The policeman's arm rose ... he held a baton ... the arm ... the baton ... was coming down.

Someone shouted next to her left ear. Someone grabbed her by the waist and pulled. The policeman's arm was gone. Someone, a boy, was dragging her so she lost her balance and stumbled, but he still pulled, hauling her through the crowd.

Suddenly he stopped. They had come around the corner of a building, in an alley, with garbage bins lined up on either side. It smelt of cockroaches and cats. Her rescuer was panting, clutching at his sides. He was a few years older than Barbara. His eyes were bright blue, gleaming under a ragged fringe of faded hair. A rough swag of clothes tied up with string rested by his ankles.

'Crikey! That was close! I thought we were for the peter then for sure.'

'The what?'

'The peter. You know, the nick, the watchhouse, gaol.'

Barbara shook her head. She tried to get the world into focus. 'Where am I? What's happened?'

'They were trying to arrest the bally lot of us,' exclaimed the boy indignantly, assuming she was talking about the demonstration they'd just left. 'Then they could kick the poor sods out. Cripes, a few blank lines in the rent book and they evict them. You a friend of theirs?' He grinned, still panting. 'You're a bit young for the UWM.'

'I don't understand.'

'The Unemployed Workers Union, chookbrain. They organised the picket.' The boy's voice shook with the remnants of anger. He wore long shorts, ragged as though they'd been cut out of trousers for some larger man, a shirt much too big for him and old-fashioned sandshoes without socks. A jumper was slung around his shoulders.

'I was just passing, but cripes, you can't walk past a thing like that. Those people had nowhere else to go. The rozzers would have put their furniture out in the street and everything. Those landlords would skin a flea for its hide ...' He caught sight of Barbara's face, which was pale with shock and fear.

'Hey, don't worry. We're out of it now.' He patted her arm awkwardly. 'We got away all right.'

What had happened? Where was she? The world was too different. The terror she had felt earlier was still there, set like concrete, with new terror piling on top. Her head felt light, as though filled with big balloons.

'What's your name, then?' The boy looked at her.

'Barbara.' Was that her voice? It sounded far away.

'Bubba what? What's up? Cat got your tongue?'

She shook her head.

'Hey.' His voice was more concerned now. 'You're as white as a sheet. That copper didn't hurt you, did he? I thought I grabbed you in time.'

'No, I ...' The world was fading again, but this was different. Her lips were cold. Everything was cold.

'Look, sit down a sec. Put your head between your knees. You're looking crook as a chook. We've got to get you home.'

'I don't have a home.' She forced her voice out.

'Everyone has a home. Where are your mum and dad?'

'No parents.' It wasn't quite a lie. Dad was gone, and Mum was ... but she couldn't think of that, she couldn't.

'Where do you live then? Where are your aunties? What about your friends? You mean you're all alone? Cripes, that's rough.'

'You don't understand.' It was suddenly so hard to speak. 'I shouldn't be here. I was somewhere else, in a demonstration.'

''Course. I was there too, remember? Look, just take it easy for a sec.'

'No!' Her tongue was getting thicker. The world was getting colder. 'It was another demonstration. Not this one.' Barbara looked around desperately. 'Where are we?'

'Sydney, of course. Are you sure that copper didn't—'

'Not *where*! I mean *when*!'

The boy stared. 'It's 1932.'

'But it can't be!'

'Well, what year do you bally well think it is?' cried the boy, exasperated.

'It's 1994.'

'Yah! You're trying to tell me you're from the future! You're as silly as a two-bob watch if you think I'm going to fall for that one.'

But his voice was growing even fainter. The cold was swallowing up the world. She closed her eyes and let the terror and the blackness fold around.

AROUND THE CORNER

There was a voice above her. Someone was holding her. Someone had wrapped her in something warm.

'Hey kid! Bubba! Hey, wake up there.'

Barbara opened her eyes. It had been a dream, a shaft of terror twisting the world out of shape.

But the strange world was still there; strange squat buildings, the smells of fermenting garbage, the strange boy holding her shoulders. She was propped against his knees and he'd wrapped something around her arms. She fingered it warily. It was the jumper he'd been wearing.

The boy was looking at her face. 'Cripes, you had me worried there for a bit,' he said. 'Hey, were you having me on before? You really think you've come from 1994?'

The cold seemed to creep all over her again. 'I don't know where I am. I don't know what's happening.'

'Well, you're not the only one.' The boy ran his fingers through his spiky hair. 'What am I going to do with you then? You think you're from the future—'

'I am!'

'Well, how did you get here then?'

'I don't know.'

Barbara shook her head desperately, trying to clear it. 'I was in this demonstration — not your one, another one — and I was scared and this old guy next to me said if I was scared just to think of going around a corner.'

'Go round a corner! What bally corner? That doesn't make sense.'

'I *know* it doesn't make sense. But I was scared. I've never been so scared before and I shut my eyes and just imagined, and then I was here.'

The boy was silent for a moment. 'You sure you didn't hit your head back there?' he finally asked.

'Of course I'm sure.'

'I wish I was,' the boy muttered, scratching his elbow. He looked at her doubtfully. 'How about you try it again then?'

'Try what?'

'This somewhere round the corner lark. Shut your eyes and think round the corner again. Maybe you'll go back to where you came from. Go on, give it a burl.'

Barbara blinked in surprise. Maybe it *would* work. Maybe it was simple. 'All right,' she said. She shut her eyes, then opened them. 'If it works — if I just disappear I mean — I want to say thank you for helping me. I don't even know your name.'

'It's Jim. Young Jim they call me. Dad's Big Jim. But don't you worry about all that now. You just shut your eyes and give it a go.'

Barbara shut her eyes. She tried to find the corner. What had it looked like? It had been so clear there at the edge of her mind. All she had to do was find the corner. She just had to walk around it and everything would be back the way it was — the screams, the terror — but she shut her mind to that. Surely she wanted to get back to the only world of her own time ... Was that the corner there? If she got a little closer she'd be sure. One step, two steps; it was so hard to move her feet. There was something wrong. It hadn't been like this before. It had been terror that had powered her feet before. She couldn't get there without terror. There'd been hands pulling her and ...

A cat screeched down the alley. The corner shimmered and was gone.

She opened her eyes. The boy — what was his name? Young Jim — was still staring at her.

'It didn't work.' Her voice was forlorn.

'I'm not bloomin' well surprised. I need my head read for suggesting it. Not that it did any harm, I suppose.' Young Jim stood up and helped her to her feet. 'Come on, hand me jumper over and stick your own on.'

Barbara handed him the jumper. 'I'm not cold now, thanks.'

'Well stick it on anyway.'

'Why?'

Young Jim looked embarrassed. He gestured around the upper part of his chest. 'Because what you're wearing—'

Barbara looked down at her T-shirt. It had a V-neck, but was perfectly ordinary. 'What's wrong with it?'

'You can see your you-know-whats through it, *that's* what's wrong! I mean, your trousers are bad enough and we don't want people staring at you. We need to be — what's the word — inconspicuous, that's it.'

Barbara blushed fiercely and fumbled as she untied her sweat-shirt from around her waist. She pulled it on roughly.

Young Jim slung his swag over his shoulder.

'Come on, we'd better get a move on.'

'But where are we going?' Barbara stumbled as she tried to catch up. Young Jim took her arm to steady her.

'Home — don't know what else I can do with you.'

'But I don't have a home, even in my own time.'

'We're going to my home. Ma will know what to do. At least she'll give you a skirt or *something* decent to wear.'

'Your home? But where is it?'

Young Jim stopped and grinned. 'Poverty Gully. The best darn dole camp in the whole of New South Wales.'

Young Jim walked fast, dodging women in high-heel shoes and shiny-seamed stockings, and men in funny hats. He had an easy lope that seemed to stretch forever. It was hard to keep up with him. It was all so small and drab and strange. It was hard not to stop and stare. The strange-looking people wearing strange clothes, the old-fashioned cars, with horses plodding among them, on funny-looking roads, the sparrows darting at the droppings, the strange signs along the street:

Depression Prices! Great bargain sale! £2,000 worth of drapery and crockery!

Gents Tailor Made Suits To Measure!

Victor Player Pianos. For Your Entertainment and Convenience!

It's Always Winter With Our New Refrigeration System!

Barbara turned her head away from the small corpses, all in rows, in the butcher's window. They were too red for chickens — rabbits maybe? There were too many questions, and no time to ask. Even the smells were odd, as if this world had never heard of underarm deodorant or the sweet cold scent of air-conditioning floating into the street.

Young Jim paused. He looked at her with concern. 'Going too fast for you?'

Barbara nodded, out of breath.

'Sorry. I'll try to go a bit slower.'

'Why do we need to hurry?'

'Well, we want to find a train round dusk, and—'

'But it won't be dark for hours.'

'Shut up and listen will you? Your mouth is robbing your ears. Poverty Gully's three to four hundred miles south of here. We can't walk all the way. Well, *I* could I reckon, but I bet *you* can't. So we're going to have to jump a train.'

'What's that mean?'

'Cripes, where have you been all your life? No, don't tell me.' Young Jim put his hand up as Barbara tried to speak. 'From somewhere round the bally corner.'

'Don't you believe me?'

Young Jim looked at her.

'No,' he said frankly. 'I reckon you got a crack on the head back there and can't think straight. But it doesn't matter. Either way you've got nowhere else to go. That means it's up to me to look after you. Ma would have my hide if I did any less.'

Young Jim took her hand and began to walk more slowly.

'Jumping a train is when you hide on a goods train or something,' he explained. 'It's what you do when you don't have the money to pay the fare. You got any money?'

Barbara shook her head. Even if she did have money, she realised, it wouldn't be worth anything here.

'Well, I've got fourpence ha'penny. That'll buy us two

tuppenny tickets to out past the goods yard. We'll hide in one of the rattlers heading south.'

'The train'll take us all the way to Poverty Gully?'

Young Jim shook his head. 'The nearest station's about fifty miles from there. We'll hail a lift if we're lucky. Otherwise it's shanks's pony.' He caught Barbara's startled look. 'We'll walk, stupid. Shanks's pony is your bally legs.'

'Fifty miles?'

'We'll get a lift,' Young Jim reassured her. 'You hungry?'

Barbara nodded. Suddenly she was starving.

'Me too. I could eat a maggoty horse as long as it had sauce on it. But we'd better save that fourpence ha'penny for the tickets.'

YOUNG JIM

The goods yard smelt of soot and coal and the hot metal of iron rails and trains. Young Jim glanced up and down the line. The girl stumbled at his side. What was her name again? Bubba, that was it. By cripes, he hoped she was all right. If only he could get her home to Ma. Ma would know what to do. Ma always did.

'Here, in this one. Quietly. I'll give you a leg up.'

'What—'

'Shhh, they'll hear us. Up on to the tarpaulin on top. Think you can make it? All right, one, two, three, heave!'

The girl scrambled onto the tarpaulin. Her hair looked like a cap around her head in the moonlight. A weird way to cut a girl's hair, thought Jim. She thrust her hand down to help him up.

'I'm right,' he grunted. 'There, we're up.' He felt around the tarpaulin and thrust his swag inside. 'Here, we'd better crawl under if we can. It'll be warmer. Less chance of being seen, too. Depends what's underneath the tarp.'

He lifted the flap and peered down. 'We don't want to be crawling in with a load of coal or superphosphate. No, it's soap. I bet there's a thousand boxes there. Sunlight, I'll bet. We'll stink like Friday night at the bathhouse by the time we get home. Come on, you get under first.'

They snuggled under the tarpaulin side by side, propping up the edge with the swag and packets of soap so they could breathe. It felt warmer immediately, though it was stuffy with the smell of soap. They lay quietly for a few minutes, listening for voices or any sign that they'd been seen.

'Jim?' Barbara's whisper was uncertain in the darkness under the tarpaulin.

'Mmmm.'

'What's a dole camp?'

'Don't you know anything? It's where you go when you don't have a house of your own and you don't have money for the rent. There's a big one out at Happy Valley and one up Newcastle way. We were there for a time. Cripes, it was crook. Everyone feeling hopeless and kids crying or playing in the dirt and everyone bitching at each other all the time. We got out of there real fast.'

'Is the place we're going like that? What did you call it, Poverty Gully?'

'Nah, the gully's not like that. It's different.'

'Jim?'

'Mmm? You can ask questions, can't you!'

'When do you think the train'll start?'

'Beats me. They weren't handing out timetables at the gate, were they? Maybe soon. Maybe not till morning.'

'What'll they do if they find us?'

'Make us get off. Might be different if we were grown up. Some of the railway dicks are supposed to be a bit rough.'

She was silent again. Young Jim shook his head in the darkness. He didn't think he'd ever been so scared as before when she'd fainted back there, with her face so white and her forehead all covered in sweat. He'd thought she'd been hurt for sure. Who *had* she been living with, anyway? Didn't they at least have some girls clothes to put her in? Didn't she have anyone to look after her except him?

'Jim? How do you know how to do this, jumping rattlers and everything?'

'Because that's how I got up to Sydney. Me and my Uncle Bill. Ma gave us money for our fares, but Uncle Bill said why waste it. So we jumped the rattler out of town. Ma would have had our hides if she'd known.'

'Where's your Uncle Bill now?'

'He's heading north with Aunty Eva. He thinks there's a chance of work up there. Maybe cane cutting, if they can get that far. I couldn't stay in Sydney by myself. I was living with them so I could go to school. There's no school in the gully and Dad wanted me to get on. Ma says I've got to get the Intermediate. Uncle Bill was going to pay my fare back to the gully, but they've hardly got tuppence to rub together, so I said I'd find my own way home.'

'He let you—'

'Well, no.' Young Jim grinned in the darkness. 'I left a note. He'll be as mad as a hornet when he finds I've gone, but there's not much he can do about it. He'll know I'll be all right. I can look after myself.'

There was a clanking up ahead. Young Jim stiffened, wondering if the train was going to start.

'What's happening? What's that?'

'Getting a full head of steam. Don't they have trains where you come from?'

'Not steam trains.'

18

She seemed matter of fact. Young Jim craned around, trying to see her face in the darkness. Surely her story couldn't be true. Nah, she'd hit her head, that's all. Or maybe she had rats in her attic, although she seemed the full quid apart from that. Young Jim wriggled back in the boxes, trying to find a comfortable position.

'Can't your uncle get a job in Sydney?'

'You kidding. What bally jobs? It's a depression.'

Barbara's voice was thoughtful beside him. 'I've heard about the Depression. Nearly everyone was unemployed, weren't they?'

'Nearly everyone *is* unemployed. You're in the middle of it now.' For a moment Young Jim wondered if she really could have ... Nah.

'About one in three, one in four, don't have jobs, they reckon. I dunno though, it seems like most people to me. That's why we're down in Poverty Gully. Dad had a job in Sydney, a real good job in a shoe factory, then it closed down. He got another job as a nightwatchman, then that place closed too. Dad thought he might have a chance panning for gold. Poverty Gully used to be a real boom town in the old days, gold mines all over the place. Dad was going to try his luck all by himself, but Ma said no, where he goes we all go.'

'Did he find gold?' Her voice sounded sleepy, nestled down in the boxes of soap.

'Nah. Not yet anyway. I reckon most of the gold was all worked out years ago. Just about everyone who comes to the gully thinks they're going to find gold. Doesn't take them long to realise it's all worked out. Only one who thinks he's going to find gold now is Gully Jack, and he's as nutty as a fruit cake. But Ma reckons there isn't much use moving on. Not till things get better. Dad put up a shack, and he's got a vegie garden going: tomatoes, cabbages like you wouldn't believe — you should see the soil down there — and there's water and all the rabbits you can trap.'

'What do you do with the rabbits?'

'Eat them, of course. Haven't you ever had a rabbit? Cripes, what I couldn't do to a roast bunny now ... and you can sell the skins, too. Poverty Gully's a real beaut place in summer, though it can be cruel in winter when the wind blows off the tablelands. I told you, the gully's not like some of those other susso camps. I wouldn't go near those with a ten-foot pole. Poverty Gully's different.'

'Why?' asked Barbara drowsily.

'What do you mean?' It had never occurred to him to question it before. 'I dunno — maybe because we're all in the same boat. I mean the farmers round there are living on the smell of an oily rag too, what with prices down and everything. They're not going to stick their noses up at someone else who's down on their luck. Maybe 'cause it's just easier living in the valley. At least there's always plenty to eat, even if it's stewed eel and tomatoes and bread and scrape ...' Young Jim paused. 'You know, I reckon it's different because we all work together. I mean, it's not like the other camps where people went because they had nowhere else to go. We all came to the gully for the gold, even if the gold isn't there. Last year when the Briars' shack blew down everyone got stuck in to build them a new one. You wouldn't see that at the other camps, I bet. Then there was last year, when Ma and Mrs Hooper made doormats out of hessian bags on Dulcie's sewing machine, and Gully Jack sold them up in town, till the machine went bung. I mean, there's always things like that going on in the gully.'

Jim waited for her to ask another question. She was always asking questions.

There was no sound beside him. She was asleep.

Suddenly the train jerked and shuddered. It began to move backwards, *clang*, then forwards, *clank*, and stopped, then began again. *Shugg shugg-u shuggu*, straining at first, as though not quite convinced that it should start at all, then gaining speed. 'What!'

'Shhh, we're off, that's all. Go back to sleep.'

He reckoned she must have been exhausted, she dropped off so quickly. He listened to her quiet breathing in the soap-scented air under the tarp, a gentle sound with the wind on top and the furious rhythm of the wheels underneath. Finally, Young Jim slept too.

He awoke at the first station, and peered up over the tarp. It was still pitch dark, the moon not yet risen. It'd be morning, he guessed, before they needed to get off. Young Jim pulled the tarp back over his head. The girl was still out to it. The train huffed like a dozing dragon. Finally it began to clank again.

Clang ... Clank ... Shugg shugg-u shuggu ...

The rhythm of the train rocked him back into an uneasy sleep, buffeted by curves and burps of smoke and the faint hiss of cinders on the tarp. The girl muttered in her sleep.

The train wheels seemed to chant her name ... BUBBA bubba BUBBA bubba BUbbubbbubbbbaaa —

Exhaustion crept over him and his breathing deepened.

'Hey, you lot! You up there! What the flaming heck do you think you're doing?'

A sharp and angry voice woke him. A hand shoved the tarp back from his face. Cold air rushed in.

The train had stopped. A man's face peered over the edge of the wagon. It was grubby, angry and dark with yesterday's whiskers.

Barbara gave a small sharp cry. Young Jim rolled in front of her to protect her. He tried to clear his head.

'Struth, it's only a couple of kids.' The anger in the man's face softened. 'I don't know what the world's coming to. Come on, out with you, you can't stay here.'

Young Jim sat up.

'Where are we?'

'Wingalooma.' The man held out his hand. He wore overalls that were black with soot and a grubby badge on his chest that proclaimed 'Lang is Right'.

'Come on, down with you.' He gave Young Jim a hand, then lifted Barbara over the edge.

Young Jim tried to calculate, rubbing the sleep from his eyes. A good two hundred miles still to go and not even near the main road. They'd never hail a ride from here.

'Are you the guard?'

'No fear, mate. I'm the fireman. There isn't a guard on this train. You should have wriggled down further, then I wouldn't have noticed you. I saw your shapes poking up under the tarp. Don't know how someone didn't pick you up before now.'

'I'll remember next time,' said Young Jim seriously.

'You'll do no such thing.' The fireman shook his head. 'Train jumping's not for kids. Don't you know it's dangerous?

A bloke got killed jumping the rattler just north of here the other day. Two other blokes got suffocated in a load of wheat last week. It's a mug's game and if you'd any sense you'd know it. Where do you think you're going anyway?'

'Home,' said Young Jim.

His voice was high with weariness. Home seemed very far away.

'Where's home then?'

'Poverty Gully. It's down from Binoweela.'

The man looked them up and down. They could see the pity spread across his face.

'Susso camp eh. Fair dinkum? That's where your parents are?'

Young Jim nodded.

The fireman rubbed his whiskery jaw. 'That's crook, that is. That's real crook.'

Young Jim glanced at Barbara. Her eyes were wide and frightened. He turned back to the fireman. 'Please don't put us off. I have to get my ... my sister home.' His voice cracked.

The fireman was silent, looking at them. He scratched his head. 'Struth, I dunno. A couple of kids. How long since you've eaten?'

'Yesterday ... I mean, the day before.' Barbara whispered.

'Struth! Hungry and shivering ... why couldn't you've jumped someone else's blooming train?'

He placed his big arm around Young Jim's shoulders. 'Come on lad, up this way. And you too, girlie. You'll be warmer along here.'

The man led them up the siding and stopped by the engine. 'Hey Charlie, get the sausages out, will you?'

The driver's head poked out, as whiskery as the engineer's, ginger streaked with grey.

'What the—'

'Couple of kids, trying to get home to that susso camp down past Binoweela. They're hungry.'

'I don't care what they are. You can't bring them up here!'

'Just for five minutes to warm them up.'

'You know the regulations as well as I do.' The angry voice was weakening.

'You can take the regulations and ... look, what'd you feel if they were your kids, eh?'

The driver looked at them sharply, then turned his back. He rummaged behind and unwrapped a thick parcel of newspaper. There were sausages in it, fat and glowing pink in the red light from the fire box. The fireman hauled himself up, grabbed the shovel and shoved it into the coals.

'Give it a minute in there and she'll be right. Come on kids, up you come. There, that's the ticket.' He flung the sausages onto the hot shovel. They wriggled fiercely and spat fat.

They smelt incredible.

'Best smell in the world, isn't it?' said the fireman. 'Nothing like it to keep you going through the small hours. Couple of snags, a bit of bread, a billy of tea and the king's your uncle. Hey, Charlie, speaking of tea ...'

The tea was hot, strong, and very sweet. The sausages were wonderful, three each, so rich they dripped into the bread. They leant into the warmth of the engine and watched the stars mingle with the sparks from the chimney overhead. Charlie ate beside them, watchful and wordless.

'Time to get moving.' The fireman put his cup down.

'Come on, you kids. There's a carriage down the end. Hop into it.'

'But—' Young Jim and Charlie spoke at once.

'Buts'll get you nowhere. If anyone asks questions, I'm paying your fare.' He glared at Charlie.

'Thank you,' whispered Barbara.

'Don't want thanks. Just you promise not to jump any more rattlers. You understand?'

'I understand,' said Young Jim quietly.

'You see that you do. And you look after your sister, too, mate. No more crazy larks like this one. Now try and get some sleep. I'll wake you at Binoweela, don't you worry.'

They walked slowly down the siding, full of sausages and kindness. They could just hear the voice of the fireman behind them.

'Only kids ... a susso camp ... you ever been to one of those places? My word, it's a fair cow.'

The carriage seats were leather, firm and soft. Young Jim tossed his swag to Barbara for a pillow, then stretched out opposite and fell asleep.

The windows were brushed with daylight when she opened her eyes. The paddocks were lush and green, with creeks like small brown snakes wriggling through their corners. Barbara huddled under Young Jim's jumper in the corner of the carriage and watched the paddocks flicker by. Young Jim was still asleep. She thought he hadn't got much sleep the night before. He was too wrapped up in looking after her.

It was a dream. It had to be a dream; or maybe the world before was the dream and the only thing real was now.

The train shuddered to a stop. Young Jim's eyes opened. He sat upright and looked out.

'Hey, we're here.'

'End of the line!' It was the fireman. He was smiling, although his face was tired and even blacker than the night before, and his eyes red-rimmed. 'Come on, home is just around the corner.'

They clambered out. The fireman shoved a couple of sandwiches at them, thick white bread oozing jam. 'They're from Charlie. He's not a bad sort really. He's just like lots of people these days, he wants to hang on to what he's got.' The fireman looked at them a bit uncertainly, 'You be all right from here?'

'We'll be right.'

'Good luck to you then.' He put out his horny hand and grabbed Young Jim's and shook it. 'You take care of your sister, too.'

Then he was gone, swinging himself up into the cab of the engine. The train began to shuffle slowly forward, then picked up speed. They watched it until only its smoke was left above the trees.

The road stretched before them, pale and dusty yellow.

'How far did you say it was?' whispered Barbara.

'Fifty miles. Nothing to it.' Young Jim grinned encouragingly. Barbara lifted her chin and tried to grin back. They crossed the railway lines and stepped onto the road.

It was cool walking at first. The magpies carolled in the tall trees scattered along the road. A kookaburra chortled, lifting its beak to the sun.

The day grew hotter. A car passed, silver-grey, leaving

a cloud of choking dust. Young Jim looked after it. 'Bunch of toffs. Flash cars never stop. I hope their tyres turn into maggots and eat their engine up for lunch. You thirsty?'

'A bit.'

'There's a creek along a way. We might take a breather there, if you like.'

It was cooler by the water. A pair of dragonflies darted through the reeds, bluer than the sky. Barbara looked at the creek doubtfully.

'You sure it's safe to drink?'

'Of course it's safe. Might taste a bit of cattle shush, but that won't do us any harm.' Young Jim bent down and scooped the water in his hand. The drips caught the light as they dribbled on his knee. Barbara knelt beside him. The water was warm, but sweet.

'If we were cockatoos we could fly across country from here,' said Young Jim, pointing. 'See that hill over there? Poverty Gully drops right down from it.'

'Why don't we go that way then?' asked Barbara, looking at the hot air shimmering above the road.

'We'd get lost. The sun'd bleach our bones before they found us,' said Young Jim cheerfully. 'Just like the old-time explorers. You learn about them at school?'

Barbara nodded. 'Will you be going to school in Poverty Gully now?' she asked.

'There isn't a school in the gully. Not for susso kids.'

'But doesn't everyone have to go to school?'

Young Jim shrugged. 'If there's a school to go to. There's a school in town. Take you a day or more to walk to it but. Kids who've got the money board in town. Come on, we'd better get moving again.'

Another car passed, then a cart. Neither stopped. The sun slipped from the centre of the sky. Barbara's feet hurt. The sausages and bread and jam had faded away, leaving her giddy from hunger and from heat. The dust seemed to fill her hair and eyes and mouth.

'Want to rest again?' Jim's eyes were dark with concern.

Barbara shook her head. What if it got dark? Would they have to sleep by the side of the road, away from everything?

'I can keep going.'

'Good girl. Look, I'll try and flag down the next car. Maybe if they see me waving they'll stop.'

Another car growled slowly up the track behind them. Barbara turned to hail it. Young Jim pulled her back. 'Not this one,' he said softly. 'We'd better let this one go.'

It was a dark green car with silver trim, open at the top, with wide thin-rimmed wheels and green spokes. The man driving it wore a sharply creased grey hat. A woman in a wide-brimmed hat trailed scarves beside him. Three children sat in the back. The car seemed so slow compared to the speeds she was used to. Barbara watched it putter up the road.

'Aren't you going to wave it down?'

'No use. That's old Nicholson. He'd run us over soon as look at us.'

'Would he really?'

'Well, perhaps not run us over. But he wouldn't pick us up, that's for sure.'

The car was nearing them. Barbara could see Nicholson's face. The lips were thin, his face sharply averted from the children by the road. The woman beside him looked into the distance as though she couldn't see them. There were three boys in the back of the car.

'Putting on the dog in a flash car,' said Young Jim loudly as the car shuddered towards them on the rough road. 'He's only a blooming shopkeeper. He's got the grocery shop down in the valley. It's the only one, so all the sussos have to get their rations there. That's how he makes his money, selling smelly cheese and stale bread to the likes of us.'

The car rumbled by. There was no sign if anyone in it had heard Young Jim's words or not. As it passed, one of the boys in the back turned around and made a rude sign through the billowing dust. The woman's head turned and the boy sat back in his seat. The car turned through some trees and was gone.

'There'll be another car,' said Young Jim reassuringly.

Step after step. The flies buzzed around her eyes and drank the sweat from her neck. Barbara kept her eyes on the road. One more step and she'd be past the pothole, one more step and she'd be past that rock, one more step ...

The noise of an engine muttered in the distance. Barbara edged to the side of the road without turning around. Why bother? It would just go past like the others, leaving the dust and fumes and emptiness.

The car stopped.

It was a police car. Barbara gasped, edging closer to Young Jim. The motor grumbled above the dusty road.

'Looking for a lift, you kiddies?'

SERGEANT RYAN

The kids stood by the side of the road.

They're as thin as matchsticks, thought Sergeant Ryan, and ragged as scarecrows, with streaks down their faces where the dust had mingled with their sweat. The girl's hair looked like a broom gone through a willy-willy and the boy didn't look much better.

What was his name? Sergeant Ryan wracked his memory. One of the O'Reilly kids from down the gully — Young Jim, that was it. He didn't recognise the girl.

There was a strange look about her, more than the tiredness and scruffiness would account for. She was wearing some bloke's pants. They looked small, though they fitted her right enough. Surely someone could have come up with a skirt for the poor kid.

'Come on, hop in if you're going to.'

'Too right!' said the boy enthusiastically. He heaved open the door. 'In you go, Bubba. This is a bit of all right, eh?'

'But ... but ...' Barbara hesitated, her eyes wide and frightened. The sergeant's eyes tightened. He wondered what she'd been through to scare her like that. It was a fair cow what some kids went through these days. If he had his way he'd—

'You going right down into the valley, Sergeant Ryan?'

The sergeant nodded. 'I'll drop you up the gully if you like. It'll be near on dark by the time we get there, anyway.'

'Come on Bubba, shake a leg.' Barbara gingerly slid across the shiny seat. She could smell the sharp scent of starch from the sergeant's uniform. A sweeter smell hovered over that. Was it hair oil, she wondered, looking at the greasy patch on the back of the seat.

'Sergeant Ryan, this is Bubba. Bubba, this is Sergeant Ryan. He's the valley's policeman.'

'For my sins,' said Sergeant Ryan. He accelerated and the car began to eat the dusty road. Slower than a normal car, thought Barbara, but fast compared to following the road on foot. Automatically, her hands fumbled around on the seat.

'Hey, keep your elbows to yourself,' ordered Young Jim. 'What're you looking for?'

'The seat belt.'

'The what?'

'The seat belt. You know.'

Young Jim shook his head. 'Never heard of it. What does a seat belt do when it's at home?'

'It stops you flinging forward when you stop suddenly or when you crash.'

Sergeant Ryan looked amused. 'Funny lot of drivers you've been riding with, love. You won't need one of those things while I'm at the wheel.'

Barbara didn't say anything. Young Jim was looking at her curiously. He started to open his mouth as though to say something, then shut it again.

Sergeant Ryan changed gears and glanced over at Young Jim.

'What are you doing back here, boy? Dulcie said you were up in Sydney working for your Intermediate.'

Young Jim shrugged. 'Uncle Bill decided to head north to look for work. What use is school anyway? There are no jobs whatever you do.'

'I don't like talk like that, son. An education's good for you, even if you never get a job in your life. But there'll be jobs again, just you wait.'

Young Jim didn't say anything. The car jolted slowly over the rutted track. Sergeant Ryan concentrated on his driving, skirting around holes so big they looked like cows had sat in them. A flat tyre'd be just what he needed now.

It had been a cow of a day. Up in town to a council meeting, and old Nicholson on at him about clearing the gully of sussos, though how he was supposed to do that he didn't know. They were camping on private property and did no-one any harm that he could see. If there were any bad eggs among them he got rid of them quick smart and he'd told Nicholson so. How could anyone look at kids like these and think to turn them out, back to places like Happy Valley or the other camps? Grim places if half of what you heard was true.

Barbara looked out at the countryside. Sheep sat like dusty rocks in the shade of trees. Suddenly the road tilted, so abruptly that it was like slipping over the edge of the world. There below them was a valley, dark blue ridges of rock and trees, with sharp squares of bright green cow-dotted paddocks and orchards and vegetable gardens. Young Jim slipped forward eagerly.

'Take a look,' he told her. 'That's the valley, down there. The gully's just up on the right. You can't see it from here.

Cripes, it's good to be coming home. You been up the gully lately, Sergeant Ryan? How's the family, and Gully Jack, and the Hendersons, and Dulcie?'

Sergeant Ryan dragged his thoughts back. 'Dulcie's still the same, bless her. I was up the gully a couple of days ago. The Hendersons are well enough. Your dad got a few of the blokes together and they built a bit of an annexe next to that tent of theirs. Henderson's all thumbs, your dad says, and he'd never have done it himself. Keeps the rain off while they're eating. Your family's doing all right, too. Dulcie said your ma's arthritis is better now that the warm weather's come. She could hardly move her hands there for a while in the cold. Your dad got a cut on his hand a couple of weeks ago stripping leaves for the eucy burners, did you know? It's healed all right now.'

'Ma wrote me. How about Gully Jack?' asked Young Jim.

'Just the same as ever,' said Sergeant Ryan, shortly.

He changed gears sharply as the hill got even steeper. He glanced at the girl by his side. She looked dead beat, with circles like saucers under her eyes, and her face as white as a pet rabbit. If she were his, thought Sergeant Ryan, he'd let her sleep for a week. He'd get her proper clothes, something frilly maybe. He imagined how Dulcie would coax soup and lamb chops with peas into her. Dulcie'd be in that apron with the flowers on it and her hair all curling at the sides of her face — that's what it would be like if Dulcie married him, and they had kids. He'd get her a gas stove so she didn't have to cart the wood, and gas light, too — no mucking about with those fool lanterns.

'Hey look, Bubba, you can see the dairy farm!' Young Jim pointed through the window. 'That's Dulcie's dairy, and the washhouse and the milking sheds, and that's the main house over there — I wonder if that's Dulcie in the paddock.'

'Who's Dulcie?' asked Barbara.

'Dulcie? Oh, Dulcie's terrific. Isn't she, Sergeant Ryan?'

'Yes,' said Sergeant Ryan.

'She owns the dairy farm; it used to be her father's. She'll do anything for anyone, Dulcie will. Ma says she doesn't know what we'd all do without her.'

'How old is she? Does she have kids too?'

'Nah, she's never married. She's pretty old but. Must be about thirty.'

'Probably,' agreed Sergeant Ryan, with the hint of a smile.

'People say she's been walking out with Gully Jack for ages, but they've never got engaged or anything. I don't think she's seen much of him lately. He's been building a new channel off the creek. Says it'll make his fortune. He doesn't seem to think of anything else.'

Barbara tried to understand. How could you make a fortune from a channel off a creek? But she was too tired to ask. Much, much too tired. She closed her eyes and dozed as the police car leant slowly around another corner. The sergeant glanced at her. The boy was too excited to notice, peering out the window, exclaiming at everything familiar he could see.

The car lumbered down into the valley. The sergeant changed gears and turned right, away from the valley proper, up towards the gully. They bumped slowly up the rutted track until it petered out. A thinner path ran through the thornbush and wattles, worn by feet, not vehicles.

'This is about as far as we go,' said Sergeant Ryan. 'You kids be all right from here?'

'We'll be all right. Hey, Bubba, wake up. We're nearly home.'

Barbara opened her eyes with difficulty. It was nearly dusk. The trees were fat with shadows. Even the track looked dark.

'Thanks, Sergeant Ryan. You saved our lives.'

The sergeant chuckled. 'You just take care now,' he said. 'No more hailing rides from strangers. If you need a lift up to town you just tell Dulcie and she'll let me know. I'll get you up there if I'm going that way, or you can take the mail car.' He slipped his hand into his pocket. 'Here, you buy yourself and the other kids some lollies next time you're down the valley.'

'Hey, sixpence! Thanks, Sergeant Ryan.'

The children walked up the winding track. The sergeant waited till they'd disappeared before he turned the car around and drove slowly back to the valley.

HOME

The track snaked through the trees. She could hear the branches rustling overhead, a gentle sound like breathing. Somewhere she could hear water, trickling over rocks and the occasional voice muffled by the wind.

'You going all right? We're nearly there.'

Barbara nodded, too tired to speak.

'He's a good bloke, Sergeant Ryan. The sergeant at the other susso camp, he was a cow of a copper. Had one poor bloke up before the magistrate just because he tried to claim the dole with five shillings on him. His ma was in the hospital and she'd sent it down so he could catch the train to go and visit her. Sergeant Ryan wouldn't do a thing like that. I reckon the gully's lucky to have him. He's been here five years now. Ma says he was transferred here when his wife died. She got an infected tooth and it killed her. He wanted a new place right away.'

'A tooth?' Barbara tried to concentrate. 'You don't die from an infected tooth. Why didn't they just give her antibiotics?'

'Anti-by-what? My Uncle George died from a bad tooth, too. They say his face swelled right up like a football or something.' Young Jim pushed a branch away from the path so Barbara could get through.

'You know, Bubba, I've been thinking. There's no point in telling Ma we jumped the rattler. I mean it'd just worry her, so I'll let her think we paid the fare. Hey, look out, we've got to cross the creek here. Give me your hand.'

The rocks were just visible in the thinning light. The creek splashed like watery oil around them. Young Jim leapt off the last rock and held out his hand to Barbara. 'The track starts just here. Be careful of that last rock, it's slippery. Got you. Come on, not long now.'

'Yuk, what's that?'

Young Jim peered down. 'That? That's just a wombat dropping. You get lots of them round here. Any high spot on a log or rock and you can bet a wombat's put its bum on it.'

Barbara looked at it uncertainly. 'Are you sure? It's pretty big.'

''Course I'm sure. We've got fat wombats round here. Lots of wombat tucker. Gully Jack reckons they're hell on the fences. He's just jealous because they're better diggers than he is.'

Something scuttled across the track. Barbara started.

'It was just a water dragon.' Young Jim's voice was reassuring in the growing dark beside her. 'You know, a lizard. You'd think it would've gone off to bed by now! They're all along the creek here. Must be hundreds of them. We'll come down and I'll show you them in the morning. There's a thousand things you'll want to see tomorrow.' He breathed deeply. 'Cripes, it's good to be back in the gully again.'

The track stretched through the trees — dark trees, with rustling tops darker than the sky. A child called somewhere in the darkness behind them, and an adult's voice echoed in the distance. The scent of smoke mingled with the smell of leaves and bark. Faint lights gleamed in the dimness from strange shapes off the track. They were too dim for electric lights, the shapes too small for proper houses.

Young Jim seemed to know his way even in the dark. They turned a corner. There was a clearing, lighter than the track under the trees. A shack was just visible at one end.

Young Jim let his breath out in relief. 'Home,' he said softly. Then more loudly. 'Bubba, we're home.'

Barbara strained her eyes in the draining light.

It wasn't what she had expected. It was just a shanty, two rooms at most, with a funny sort of flat verandah out the front propped up by wattle poles with peeling bark. The whole structure seemed to be made of branches, still rough with bark, the cracks plugged up with clay. The roof was pieces of tin all hammered flat. It shone in the last of the light. The remains of a fire glowed out the front. There was no front door. Someone pushed an old sack aside and stood there, holding up a lantern. It was hard to see the face behind the light.

'Who is it?'

'Ma! It's me!'

The distant figure gave a cry and ran forward. Young Jim ran too. The lantern light shuddered, as she hugged him hard.

'You should have told us you were coming home. Where's Bill?'

There were more voices now, erupting from the shanty.

'Hey, it's Young Jim—'

'Jim, Jim, did you bring me anything—'

'Why didn't you *say* you were coming home?'

'Now don't tell me Bill let you come all this way alone?' That was a man's voice.

'Hey, Young Jim, I've lost another tooth, see—'

'I'll have his guts for garters, you see if I don't!'

'It wasn't his fault, Dad.'

'Young Jim, hey Young Jim, that old cow of Dulcie's had another calf, the splotchy one.'

'Who's this?'

It was a girl's voice. Someone lifted up the lantern. Barbara blinked as the light hit her eyes. There seemed to be dozens of people in the clearing, kids mostly, with bare feet and limp thin clothes. They were all staring at her.

'Is she a friend of yours, Young Jim? Where'd she get those clothes?'

'What's her name?' It was a small girl who spoke, her eyes reflecting the night.

'Why, the poor lamb, she looks done in.' It was Ma; she wrapped her arms around Barbara, strong and soft.

'Elaine, you help Young Jim to make a bed up. Dad, you go and look for something warm. Someone get some water, will you? And Joey, stoke up the fire and put the billy on please. If there was ever a time we needed a bit of tea ...'

The world was blurred, but comforting. The voices were blurred as well.

'Who are her people, then?' A man's voice.

'I don't know and I don't care. As long as we've got a roof over our heads and a bit in the pot I'll not be turning any child away.'

'Look, love, I didn't mean ... of course she can stay. Who am I to object? You're the one who manages things, not me. You can feed the whole world if you want to.'

Then there was nothing but the feel of a mattress beneath her, hard, but infinitely welcoming, the warm voice murmuring comfort. Then there was sleep.

POVERTY GULLY

There were voices outside.

'Ma, Thellie's got my best rabbit snare and won't let go.'

'It's mine, I made it.'

'Did not!'

'Did so too! Last Tuesday, you ask Elaine if you don't believe me.'

'What would she know anyway? Ma, it's mine.'

'Keep your voices down, can't you! Bubba's trying to sleep in there.'

It was a voice she knew. Young Jim, from yesterday. Could it be only yesterday she had met him? He'd told the engine driver that she was his sister and a glow had spread right through her, as though she really did have a family, a real one of her own.

'When's she going to wake up?' That was one of the younger voices again. Young Jim said something, too soft for her to hear. There was a scuffle, then they seemed to move away.

Barbara looked around. It was hard to see anything in the dark room. She was on a bed, close to the ground: a home-made mattress on top of a base of boxes. She could just see the shapes of other beds around the room, spread with blankets made of hessian sacks sewn together, and

41

something that looked like rough-tanned furs. There was one window — just a hole without any glass at all — covered with a sort of sacking blind. The only light in the room seeped around the sacking blind and the curtain-covered doorway, and through the chinks in the walls and roof.

She sat up carefully. The floor was dirt, packed hard and swept so there was no dust. Someone had taken her jeans and shoes and put her in a dressing gown which was far too big, and socks, thick with darning, on her feet.

It was easier to see now as her eyes adjusted to the darkness. Her head bumped on the ceiling. It must be far too low for Young Jim. She pushed aside the sacking curtain and found herself in the open air, under the verandah-like annexe.

The world was leaves and sky and the low, sweet hush of trees. A fire smouldered in a rough stone fireplace with a big tin on one side. The smoke rose slowly and sifted across the valley, directionless without a breeze. The ground was bare, as though trodden clear by many feet.

'About time you were up.' The voice startled her. A man was watching from the corner of the verandah, sitting on a rough chair made of some sort of skin suspended between two bits of wood. He got to his feet slowly. He was very tall and thin, with tattered shorts that came nearly to his bony knees and whiskers in all shades of grey and brown tattered around his chin. He put out a hand, as large and knobbly as the rest of him.

'I'm Jim. Pleased to meet you.'

'Jim? I thought Jim was—'

'That's my boy, Young Jim. I reckon that makes me

Old Jim. Good-for-nothing Jim. They call me Big Jim, though. It sounds better than good-for-nothing Jim, but I reckon it means the same. Or Dad of course. That's what you'd better call me too, I reckon, if you're going to be staying here.' He squatted down on the rough seat, his big knees nearly touching his chin. 'And you're Bubba. Young Jim told me about you last night. You feeling better now?'

Barbara nodded. 'I think so. Much better. I'm sorry to be a nuisance.'

Dad laughed. It was a short laugh, with bitterness not far away. 'You're not a nuisance, girl. Struth, there's so many kids around here one more won't make any difference. Bit like a mob of bandicoots, you never know where one'll pop up next.' He looked at her closely. 'Young Jim said you haven't got any family. That right? What happened to them, then? You haven't been running away from home have you?'

'No ...' Barbara's voice choked.

''Cause the way I see it, if you've got folks looking for you we've got to write them a letter or something, to let them know you're safe. So you tell me honestly. Is there someone wondering where you are?'

Barbara shook her head.

'You telling me the truth, Bubba?'

'Yes. There's no-one who'll be looking for me. I promise. No-one who'll miss me. I ...' Suddenly the memories came rushing in. She shut her eyes as though to drive them away.

Suddenly Dad's arm was around her shoulders.

'All right love. Don't say nothing if it upsets you. All right now? Struth, I reckon I've got secrets of my own I don't want nobody to know about. You dry those tears, okay? Because I reckon it's nearly lunchtime and the whole mob'll be in and we want you looking like roses and cream or Ma will want to know why. She's the salt of the earth, that woman, but she's got a tongue about her, and I don't think I could take it today, not before I've had me lunch anyway. So no more tears, you hear?'

Barbara nodded. She tried to smile.

'Put it here,' said Dad, putting out his hand. 'Who am I to be making judgments on anyone? Mates, all right?'

Barbara nodded again, grateful. She sniffed and glanced at the dressing gown. She couldn't wipe her nose on someone else's sleeve. Dad pulled out a handkerchief.

'Go on, blow. It's clean. Now you go get some clean clothes on. They're spread out in the other room waiting for you, and then sit down before the littl'uns grab the best seats in the house. We'll see if Ma has rustled up something for lunch except for bread-and-duck-under-the-table. Off you pop.'

Lunch was rabbit stew from the iron pot on the fire, full of little bones and chunks of squishy carrot; six giant spoonfuls for everyone, measured exactly by Ma and her ladle, with butterless scones from the big tin oven.

The stew was stringy, but tasty; hot and full of meat. The scones were wonderful, although it was funny to eat them soaked with stew, and not with butter, or jam and cream. The little ones yelled and chattered through the meal, picking at the sodden scones and shreds of meat with their fingers. Only Ma and Dad had forks, though Young Jim had a knife he kept on his belt.

'You had enough, Bubba?'

Ma scraped around the edges of the pot with her ladle. Like the kids she had bare feet, tough and brown and splayed at the toes, dirty to the ankles. Her brown hair was clean, though, and shone like the sun on the flat tin roof. It was tied back in a ponytail with a bit of string.

Barbara nodded. 'Thank you. I'm full.'

'Give it here then Ma!'

'No, here!'

'You shut your mouths before the flies fly in. If Bubba doesn't want it I'll give it to your dad. There's one more scone each if you're hungry and tomato jam in the box, but only one spoonful, mind, and there are little apples in the box from Dulcie's. You're sure you can't eat it, love? You could do with a bit more meat on your bones. You look like a match with the wood scraped off.'

'She looks all right. Better than last night anyway.' Young Jim grinned across the old door propped up on rocks that served as a table. 'You lay off her, Ma. At least she's got a bit of colour in her cheeks again.'

Barbara smiled back. She did feel better. Things were strange, but there was nothing to be scared of here.

'I saw Sergeant Ryan down on the track before lunch,' said the biggest of the girls. What was her name? Yes, Elaine. She was about Barbara's age, or maybe a year older. A bit like a freckled banana, thought Barbara, with her hair streaked brown and yellow, and dark deep eyes.

Elaine chewed on a rabbit bone thoughtfully.

'He wanted to know if Jim and Bubba got here safely. He said to tell Dad there might be some relief work next month on the roads up near town. He said we could send

Young Jim down as well, if we want. He'd pass him as eighteen.'

'I don't want any son of mine working the relief,' said Dad, shifting on his wooden seat. 'One good-for-nothing in this family is enough. Young Jim should be in school. That's where the lot of you should be.'

'Sergeant Ryan's a good man,' said Ma sharply. 'You don't get them better than Sergeant Ryan. The relief work'll be easier on your back than the eucy cutting, and there'll be more money in it too. Clean out the pan will you, Elaine love, and put the water on. My tongue's just hanging out for a cup of tea.'

Barbara sipped the tea slowly. It was hot and very sweet, but weak, made from damp tea leaves Ma had taken from a can in an old safe at the back of the verandah. She watched the others chatter and dribble golden syrup on scones. No-one except the ants had touched the tomato jam.

Ma and Dad talked least: Ma because she was mostly busy, making tea or spooning food into the little ones, wiping noses, apportioning out the syrup and the scones; Dad because he just sat watching the smoke, and letting the talk flow past him.

Elaine talked most, chattering to Young Jim, and Jim talked too, telling them about Sydney and the harbour bridge, the eviction and the demonstration, about the Unemployed Worker's Union and about people she'd never met. The little ones listened, their mouths stuffed full of food — Harry, with his bum still bare and his bulging toddler's belly; Thellie, a couple of years older, a thin face with big eyes and a funny toothy smile; and Joey somewhere in between, with his long legs in baggy shorts that looked like they'd been cut down from trousers for a much larger man.

Elaine wiped the gravy from her plate with the last scone crumbs and glanced over at Barbara. 'You've never told us how you met Bubba,' she said to Young Jim.

'At the demonstration,' Young Jim grinned at Barbara over the little ones' heads.

'What was she doing there?'

'What were *you* doing there, I'd like to know,' put in Ma. She brushed a stray bit of hair back from her forehead. 'I'll skin that Bill alive, you see if I don't. He said he'd keep an eye on you, him and Eva, and look what happens.'

'Hey, Ma, it wasn't Uncle Bill's fault,' soothed Young Jim. 'Anyway, Bubba didn't have anywhere to go, so I—'

'Why not?' This was Elaine again. 'They evict you too? Where's your home then?'

Everyone was silent, watching. Barbara took a breath. 'I don't know,' she said. 'Something weird happened. I'm really from the future.'

'You're what?' Elaine giggled.

'I, ah, there was a demonstration, and this old man said ...' Barbara's voice shook as she explained it all again.

There was silence when she'd finished. Barbara waited for Elaine to giggle. Young Jim spoke firmly, 'She was hit on the head by that flaming copper. That's what I reckon.'

'No swearing,' said Ma. She put her arm around Barbara's shoulders and hugged her. 'It doesn't matter where you're from, love. You're safe here now. You're one of us now. You understand?'

Barbara looked around at the other faces. Young Jim was grinning at her, and Big Jim too. The little ones were wide-eyed. Even Elaine was smiling.

'You can come from the moon for all I care,' she said frankly. 'It's about time there was someone decent around here to talk to. There's been no-one my age at all since the Briars moved away.'

Young Jim grabbed her hand. 'Come on,' he said. 'Let's get some water for Ma and then we'll show you round.'

'You have a good wash down the creek while you're at it,' Ma called after them. 'Looks like you're wearing half the dirt of Sydney on your backs!'

DOWN THE GULLY

The creek glistened like silver paper, threaded with little streams of mud washed down by people panning further upstream. An old man crouched among the boulders, a hessian sack around his shoulders for warmth against the cold of the water, a tin plate tilted in his hand. He waved to the children, then bent down to his plate again.

'That's Old Man Lee,' said Elaine. 'He's always at it.'

'What's he doing?' asked Barbara.

'Gold-panning, of course. That's his spot. Johnny Parker and the Williams boys are up by the island. Johnny Parker was a carpenter till his shop went bust, and Joe Williams was a boilermaker. There are prospectors all up and down the creek round here. Not that there's much to be found any more. Dad says they're lucky to make half a quid a week.'

'Where's Dad panning now?' asked Young Jim.

Elaine shrugged. 'Nowhere much. The last spot fizzled out after a couple of weeks. He hasn't found another good one. Don't think he will, either. He's making a few bob out of tomatoes. Says there's more money in vegies than fooling around looking for gold, if only he could get the water to them.' Elaine grimaced. 'Boy, am I sick of

49

tomatoes. We've had them fried just about every day this month. When I grow up I'm never going to eat a tomato ever again. Or wipe a kid's grubby face, either.'

Barbara stared at the cold figure down by the creek, huddled over his pan as if it might keep him warm. 'How do you gold-pan?'

'It's easy.' Elaine pantomimed holding a flat dish. 'You just scoop up some sand and some water and keep washing out the loose stuff. Gold's heavier than sand, so what you've got left at the end'll be gold.'

'You hope,' said Young Jim.

Elaine made a face. 'You hope,' she agreed. 'Mostly you just get frozen fingers and empty pockets. Gold panning's not bad in summer, but it can be cruel in winter. Susie Briar's dad nearly lost his arm, he got so cold, and not much to show for it. Mostly all that's in your pan is gravel and fool's gold. Real gold glows even in the shade.'

'Then you stick it in a jam-jar and hope you find some more,' said Young Jim. 'But mostly you don't. Hey, look over there! I said I'd show you dragons!' Young Jim pointed at a hump of rock that sliced the flashing water of the creek.

'What is it?' Barbara had nearly forgotten his promise from the night before.

'Water dragons. See? Look at that one — he must be as long as my arm!'

Barbara blinked. Suddenly she could see what had been camouflaged before — a lizard on the rock, with its face to the sun, too intent on soaking up the heat to notice them. Its body was dull olive, with dark and light mottles, its throat a flash of red and iridescent green. It only needed wings, and fiery breath to match its throat, to be a dragon from a fairy tale.

'Come on,' said Elaine. 'Time to wash. I'll keep a lookout to make sure no-one comes by. You can use this pool and Young Jim can go and bathe around the bend.'

'Hey, no fair! This pool's warmer,' protested Young Jim.

'So sucks boo to you. You can go back and wait till Bubba's finished if you like.'

'Nah.' Young Jim bundled up his clean clothes. 'Give me a hoy when you're through, will you? And don't be long. There's loads of things I want to show Bubba today.'

Barbara looked at the creek threading through smooth pink granite rocks, purple cold in the shade of the tall casuarinas, gold and silver where it caught the light. It seemed a long way from neat blue swimming pools or hot showers in the bathroom. She waded in ankle-deep and shivered, looking at the gooseflesh on her arms and legs.

'It's freezing!'

Elaine laughed from the bank. 'Told you so. You get used to it. It's awful in winter. You can feel the bits of ice nibbling at your toes.'

'Don't you have a bathroom at all that you can use?' demanded Barbara.

''Course not. You saw our place. Where'd we put a bathroom? Behind a blinkin' tree? Ma boils up water for a hot bath on Fridays before the dance, that's all. We wash down here the rest of the time.' Elaine sighed. 'It's my job to bath the littl'uns after breakfast. Takes half the blessed morning. Hey, be careful with that soap. Soap doesn't grow on trees, you know.'

'Sorry, I didn't think.' Barbara laid the soap carefully on a bit of bark on the bank. It was a funny-shaped ball, a bit grubby, as though it had been made from soap scraps all stuck together. 'Maybe Jim'll help you wash the littl'uns now he's back.'

Elaine snorted. 'In a pig's eye. Ma gives him other jobs, like collecting wood and things like that. Fun things. She says looking after kids is a woman's job. Says it'll teach me to look after my own. Huh. Pigs'll fly before I have a pack of grubby brats to wash.'

'That's silly,' said Barbara. She caught the bit of hessian Elaine tossed her for a towel. It was soft and absorbent from lots of washing. 'There's no such thing as women's work and men's work. They should both look after the kids.'

'Maybe where you come from.' Elaine looked at her curiously. 'You're really serious with this around the corner lark, aren't you?'

Barbara nodded. She began to dress. The clothes felt soft and thin and faded and they were much too big. Her skin tingled after the cold water, as though warmed by an inner sun.

'Well,' said Elaine, 'all I can say is, if boys have to help look after the kids and things like that, I like the sound of it. I've had it up to here with looking after little kids. You decent yet? I'll give Young Jim a hoy. He'll be dressed. He only ever gives himself a lick and a promise anyway.'

They walked slowly back up the hill, Young Jim carrying the water up from the creek in two big tins that had once held kerosene. His neck bowed with the weight of them and the muscles strained in his arms.

'Let me help,' offered Barbara. 'Maybe if Elaine and I carried one between us.'

Young Jim shook his head, too out of breath to talk.

'You let him be a he-man if he wants to,' advised Elaine, picking her way beside them. 'I've had to carry those bally cans every day while he was gone. I could only manage one at a time, too.' She kicked at a bare root in the eroded path with her toe. 'When we lived in town we had running water and electric light and everything.'

'Doesn't anyone here have electricity?'

'Nah, of course not. Where'd they get electricity from? The pub's got a generator, but it goes off at closing time. That's how Sergeant Ryan can tell if there's any drinking after hours — he just listens for the generator. Not that I'd reckon he'd do much anyway. Sergeant Ryan never arrests anyone.'

'Why not?'

'He'd have to feed them if he locked them up, and he can't cook! If there's anyone he doesn't like the look of he just gives them the word to leave the valley. Mrs Cooper down at the pub takes him his meals, and I think he goes down to Dulcie's sometimes, too. Dulcie'd feed a bandicoot if it was hungry.'

'I bet Gully Jack's not too keen on that,' remarked Young Jim.

'Huh,' said Elaine. 'I bet he doesn't even notice. He's too busy with his latest channel. He wouldn't notice if a circus came to town.'

'Who's Gully Jack?' Barbara remembered the name. What was it Jim had said? Something about channels and making his fortune.

'Gully Jack's beaut. Hey, Jim, how about we take Bubba down to Gully Jack's? You haven't seen his latest channel.'

Young Jim nodded as he lifted the tins again.

The shanty came into sight as they crested the hill. Barbara thought it looked even smaller than it had the night before, but homier somehow. The little ones were playing some game in the trees behind it, with Harry trying to join in. Dad was in the vegetable patch, chipping at the ground with an old hoe. Ma looked up from kneading dough on the makeshift table. She smiled wearily when she saw them.

'Put the water over there, would you love? And throw a stick of kindling on the fire. I want to get a bit of damper cooked when the coals are right.'

'Better get going before she finds something else for us to do,' whispered Elaine. 'Like look after the littl'uns.'

'I wouldn't mind looking after the kids,' offered Barbara.

'I would. Come on.' Elaine ran off along the track.

GULLY JACK

The track wound between clearings, each carved out between the trees, with a shack or tent or sometimes both in every one; shacks of hammered kero tins or lean-tos of wattle poles with mud and hessian stretched between, of rough sawn poles or scavenged bits of timber or battered corrugated iron. Some were substantial and had two or even three rooms and a verandah, with hand-cut casuarina shingles carefully layered on the roof; some were simply lean-tos that looked like a breeze would blow them over.

Most of the clearings had gardens, neat rows of long green leaves and ferny tops, or long straight rows of corn, the ground spread thick with old cow droppings or freshly dug. Chooks clucked from a makeshift run of bark and wattle branches. An elderly man was carefully watering seedlings from a tin like the ones Young Jim had carried; a faded woman nursing a small baby waved from a lean-to further on.

'That's Mrs Hester's latest,' explained Elaine. 'Dulcie made her stay at the dairy farm to have it last week. She had her in the best spare room. The doctor came and everything.'

'Who paid the doctor then?' demanded Young Jim. 'Not Dulcie.'

'Of course not. Dulcie doesn't have money like that. I bet it'd cost you five pounds to have a doctor for a baby. I don't suppose Dr Green charged her anything. He's a good bloke. He didn't charge anything when Thellie got sick last winter, either.'

'What was wrong with her?' asked Barbara, remembering Thellie's dark eyes and too thin wrists and ankles.

'Dr Green said pneumonia. She was awfully sick for a while. Ma sat up with her every night for weeks. Dr Green said it was the cold and damp that did it. The wind just whistles through our place in winter. Couple of kids down the valley died of it. It's a killer, that wind.'

'Is she all right now?'

'A bit thin, that's all. Dr Green brought her up a tonic when he stitched up Dad's hand after he sliced it open eucy cutting.'

'What's eucy cutting?' Barbara ducked under a low hanging branch.

'Don't you know anything? It's cutting down the young saplings and branches to make eucalyptus oil. They boil up all the leaves and skim the oil off. Hey, see that tree? There's a wild bees' nest around the back. Gully Jack got some honey out of it last week. He gave us a chunk of honeycomb. My word it was good. Morning Mr Henderson,' she yelled brightly.

A tall square man with a face like a sad cow nodded from the woodpile in front of a tent, then turned back without meeeting their eyes. His clothes looked like they had once been good, though the trousers now bagged at the knees. His collar was frayed along the seams and one shoe gaped at the toe. Even the tent looked like it had been good once, with proper poles and guy ropes. It was patched now and weathered. It looked too thin to survive another storm. A rough shelter of four poles roofed with interwoven leaves and branches stood beside it. A woman sat in its shade, pulling wool out of an old jumper and rolling it into a ball. She looked as though she was about to say something, then glanced at her husband. She smiled at the children instead of speaking.

The man looked up suddenly, as though really seeing the children for the first time. He straightened unconsciously. It was as though he almost became someone else. 'It's Young Jim O'Reilly, isn't it?' he demanded. 'I thought you were up in Sydney getting yourself an education.'

'I was,' explained Young Jim. 'But Uncle Bill decided to go up north, so I had to come back here.' He shrugged. 'Don't suppose an education would have done me much good anyway.'

The man opened his mouth, as though he was going to say something, then changed his mind. His body slumped. He nodded again abruptly and turned back to the woodpile, stacking it inexpertly into a neater heap.

'That is the first time I've heard Mr Henderson say anything to anyone for weeks,' declared Elaine, as they turned the corner, out of hearing. The creek bubbled beside the path now, cold and silver between its stones. 'Usually he just keeps his mouth shut and looks the other way, like he hopes you'll think he's not there or something. He used to be headmaster up at Hastings River.'

'What happened?' Barbara stepped over a pile of flood debris, sticks and leaves jammed up against an eroded root and crowned with wombat droppings.

'They closed down the school there. They're laying off teachers all over the place so he couldn't get another job and the house went with the school.'

'What about his wife? Didn't she have a job?'

'She used to be a teacher too, but of course she had to give it up when she got married.'

Barbara stared. 'Why?'

'Well, you can't have women taking men's jobs, can you?' explained Young Jim reasonably.

'It shouldn't matter *who* has the job, the man or the woman,' said Barbara.

Elaine giggled. 'You tell him, Bubba. Hey, there's Gully Jack. Cooee! Jack!'

Barbara squinted in the dappled light. At first there seemed to be no-one in sight. Then something bobbed up from behind a fallen log. It was the top of a hat, battered and stained the same colour as the tussocks.

'He can't hear you down there,' said Young Jim.

'He's always down that channel. Ma says he'll turn into a wombat one day! Cooee, Jack! Young Jim's home!'

The channel was more obvious as they drew closer — a sudden plunge down a bank, a bit wider than a man could stretch his arms, and carefully lined with granite rocks from the creek. A face peered out from under the hat, blue-eyed and streaked with dirt, on top of bare brown shoulders shiny with sweat and dappled with dirt. Gully Jack's teeth flashed white in his dirty face. 'With you in a sec, kids.'

He put his hands up on the bank of the channel. His body followed his hands. Barbara stared. She'd never seen anyone haul themselves up with their hands, except in a circus.

Gully Jack was taller even than Dad. He had black hair and eyes that seemed to smile and dream. His arms were thick as wattle trunks, thought Barbara. His hands looked big enough to juggle granite boulders.

Gully Jack dusted his hands on his muddy trousers and lifted his shirt off a thornbush. 'When did you get back, Young Jim?' he inquired, thrusting his arms into his shirt and doing up the three buttons that were left on it.

'Last night. Gully Jack, this is Bubba. She's living with us now. Hey, is that your new channel?'

Gully Jack nodded, his eyes gleaming. Barbara peered down. The channel cut across a bend in the creek, almost making an island of the bank. It was deeper than she was tall. Stones were fitted together like a jigsaw puzzle halfway up the sides. Each end was stopped with thin walls of untouched dirt to stop the creek water running in.

'A beaut, isn't it?' demanded Gully Jack proudly. 'I think this'll be the one that does it. We'll be piling gold dust down on the bank counter yet, you wait and see.'

Barbara looked from one to the other. 'I really don't understand,' she said slowly. 'How does a channel help you find gold?'

Gully Jack laughed. 'It's like this,' he told her eagerly. 'You see that bank over there? That's where I reckon the gold is.' He waved his hands enthusiastically. 'I reckon a thousand years ago the creek flowed over here, where I'm digging, and was diverted by a flood. That bank was left by the flood. The creek'd have had gold in it then too. Reckon it dumped the gold in that bank all those years and years ago and it's still waiting for us now.'

'But why the channel? Wouldn't it be easier just to

dig down there?' Barbara gazed down at the careful stonework, the deep walls that must have taken months of work to build.

'Nah.' Gully Jack was scornful. 'If there was a seam of gold down there, that's where I'd be digging. I'd be plucking out the nuggets before you could say Jack Robinson. But that gold's alluvial. It's all in little flecks. To get it out I need water, lots of water, a whole blasted creek of it. When I get this stonework built right up to the top of the bank, I'll dig that last bit out by the creek and the whole lot'll come flooding in. That way I'll have all the water I need.'

'If we don't have a flood and it all washes away first,' pointed out Elaine.

Gully Jack grinned. 'That's what happened to me last time,' he admitted. 'I've left a bigger bank by the creek this time. I reckon she'll hold except in a real bank-to-banker.'

Barbara gazed at him, wondering what sort of person could imagine the gold under the ground and change a whole creek to get to it, with nothing but a mattock and a barrow and his calloused hands. 'Do you think you'll get a flood like that?' she asked.

'Who knows?' Gully Jack wiped his hands again, adding to the burden of mud on his trousers. 'Only God and the cockatoos, and neither of them's telling.' He glanced at the sky. 'Time to put the billy on,' he announced. 'I could eat the leg off an elephant. You three kids want to join me?'

'Too right,' agreed Young Jim.

Elaine and Barbara nodded.

Gully Jack led the way along the track to the next

clearing. It was large, two cleared paddocks, and behind them were others starting to regrow wattle trees and thornbush, properly fenced with slabs of wood, though many had sagged or were broken. A mob of sheep grazed half-heartedly, casting covetous looks at the straggly vegetable garden on the other side of the fence. A fat horse snickered at them from under the shade of a wattle.

The house itself was in the same condition as the fences. Once solid and substantial, the verandah now leant on one side under the weight of a jasmine vine, and a couple of the stairs were missing. A black and white dog lay across the front door. It opened one eye at them, then went back to sleep.

Gully Jack stepped over him. 'Watch out for Joe Blakes,' he told them. 'There was a big fat bloke sunning himself by the front door this morning. This lazy coot didn't even raise an eyelid to scare him off.'

'Who's Joe Blakes?' whispered Barbara.

'Snakes, cabbage brain,' Elaine whispered back. 'It rhymes — snake, Joe Blake — you get it?'

Barbara nodded as Gully Jack led them down a narrow hallway. The walls were covered with brown and cream wallpaper, though it was hard to make out which was the pattern and which were stains. Doors opened to dusty rooms. Barbara peered into them. There were beds with bare mattresses, a dog-haired sofa with bulging springs, the dining room with brown and purple paintings hung on the walls, a giant antique table, candles on the sideboard and torn and faded curtains at the windows.

'How many people live here?' she whispered.

'Me and I and no-one else. In here, kids.' Gully Jack

took his hat off and hung it on a hook beside the door, where it clung like a soggy mushroom against the faded paint. 'I'm as hungry as a mob of cockies in a walnut tree. Reckon I was so busy out there I forgot to come in for me dinner.'

The kitchen was at the back of the house, stretching all the way across it. Long windows ended at bench level, with wooden shutters clanging gently. Unlike the rest of the house it looked lived in — mud was ground into the torn lino floor, a dresser held a few chipped plates and a stack of saucers, all intact and evidently never used. A frying pan half-full of congealed fat sat on a black, iron, wood-fired stove, and a long wooden table, scarred with age, bore a chipped brown teapot and a pile of dirty cups that matched the saucers.

In the middle of the table, under a fly-proof cage, were the remains of a loaf of black-crusted white bread, and a leg of mutton, its side well gashed, oozed yellow dripping onto its plate. An open pot of chutney stood next to it. Barbara peered dubiously into the chutney.

'Sit yourselves down,' said Gully Jack. 'There's nothing like work to give a man an appetite.' He began to carve the bread with an old handleless breadknife.

'Have to get this fixed one of these days,' he said. 'Never seem to have the time.' He shrugged. 'When my boat comes in I'll buy a hundred breadknives if I want to.'

He sniffed the mutton. 'Still good,' he decided. 'That's the great thing about mutton — it'll last you for days. I cook a couple of legs and some chops once a week or so, and it lasts till Sunday, as long as the flies don't get it first.' He began to carve the mutton, great fat slabs almost as thick as the bread. He slapped them together, fished a fly out of the chutney and flicked it out the window, then liberally spread the mutton with the shiny brown paste.

'Get stuck into it,' he said. 'One word's as good as ten, bog in, Amen.'

Elaine giggled. Young Jim raised an eyebrow at her. 'If Ma hears you saying that instead of proper grace she'll have your hide,' he told her.

Elaine sniffed. 'You think I'd repeat that at home? I've got more sense than some people I could name. Who was it told Ma that—'

'No squabbling at the table, kiddies,' ordered Gully Jack. 'You'd give a bloke indigestion.'

'Who's a kiddie?' demanded Young Jim.

'Well, don't blasted act like one,' Gully Jack advised him. He bit into his bread, getting half of it in his mouth with one bite. Barbara watched amazed as he finished it in two gulps more and began to hack the loaf again. Gully Jack saw her stare.

'Hey, what's the matter? Get your teeth into it. That's good tucker. The flies'll finish it before you do.'

Barbara took a cautious bite. It was good, much better than she expected. The bread was tasty, even if a bit stale, and the meat was tender. Even the chutney tasted okay.

'Go on, line your belly,' Gully Jack told her. 'Plenty more where that came from.' He reached for the teapot and poured himself a cup, deep black, with tea leaves floating on top.

'Anyone else for a cuppa?' he asked.

'Isn't it cold?' asked Barbara.

Gully Jack shrugged. 'Who's got time to boil the billy

every time you want a cup of tea? If I did that I'd spend my life watching the stove. Not to mention chopping wood. Nah, this'll do me fine. Made it last night and drank it for breakfast and it's just as good now. Long as it's sweet and wet.'

'You going to be playing the fiddle at the dance this Friday?' asked Elaine.

''Course I'll be fiddling,' said Gully Jack through another mouthful of bread and meat. 'How'd you lot dance if I didn't?'

'Mrs Reynolds plays the piano. We could ask her.'

'Old Ma Reynolds plays like an arthritic chook,' declared Gully Jack. 'Plunk, plonk, plonk. As long as they give me my whisky I'll keep on playing.' He turned to Barbara and explained. 'That's all I need — whisky once a week to help me digestion, and three good meals a day. Grow my own vegies, though the weeds are getting into them a bit, and kill a sheep now and then. Killed one yesterday so, if you kids remind me, I'll give you a forequarter to take up to your Ma.' Gully Jack glanced at the slab of meat on his table, congealed in its fat and cindered around the edges. 'I bet she'll cook it real good, too. You kids are lucky with a cook like your Ma. I wish I had someone like that to cook for me.'

He stretched his big arms up towards the ceiling, yawned and rubbed his whiskers. 'I've got enough gold dust in the jar under the floorboards to buy my bread and cocky's joy. I've got a roof over my head and last week's newspaper in my dunny. And one day I'll find that gold. What more does a bloke need?'

Gully Jack wiped his mouth with the back of his hand

and stood up. The fire was in his eyes. His hands twitched, as though they couldn't wait to grasp the stones again.

'You'd never think he owned half the gully, would you?' said Elaine, as they walked back up the hill with the meat he'd given them swinging in an old flour sack. She stroked the bunch of hydrangeas 'for your Ma' that Gully Jack had grabbed on the way out the door and thrust into Elaine's hands. 'I reckon Gully Jack's the only man in the valley who'd pick a bunch of flowers.'

'Do you think he'll really find gold?' asked Barbara.

Elaine laughed. 'Gully Jack? Nah. He's got bats in his belfry, that's all. He's built gullies all along the creek and not one of them has struck gold. His dad was just the same, silly as a two-bob watch, and his uncle too. All this,' she gestured at the tangle of wattles and thornbush on either side, 'they just let it go for years. It used to be a dairy farm as good as Dulcie's, but you'd never know it now.'

'Who *is* Dulcie?' asked Barbara.

'Dulcie? Everyone knows Dulcie. How about we dump this lot and I'll take you down to meet her.'

'Oh no, you don't,' ordered Young Jim. 'You'll stay put and give Ma a hand with the littl'uns. It's too late to take Bubba traipsing all the way down there. She's still bushed from yesterday. You let her rest.'

'What about you then?' demanded Elaine.

'I promised I'd get some firewood,' Young Jim reminded her. 'And Ma will need more water.'

'I could get the water,' offered Barbara shyly.

'Good-oh. I want to go and see if there's anything in my rabbit snares. We'll see Dulcie tomorrow anyway. It's Thursday, remember.'

'What's so special about Thursdays?' inquired Barbara.

Elaine stared at her. 'It's the day you get the dole rations. I thought everyone knew that.'

Barbara was silent. Elaine shrugged. Young Jim hesitated.

'You'll be right,' he said finally. 'You'll remember soon enough.'

The three of them clambered up the path, past the shanties beneath the trees, to the billow of white smoke that meant home.

A STORY FROM AROUND THE CORNER

Fog was sifting up the valley with the dusk, soft white streaks above the edges of the creek. The light was thick with dew and shadow. Barbara sat by the creek with the empty kero tin beside her and watched the dark smooth water-creases slipping towards the sea.

Was it real? Could she just slip back without warning? How firmly was she held in this world around the corner?

She had to see. She had to be sure.

Barbara shut her eyes. She tried to imagine the corner. She tried to see her feet walking towards it. She tried to see around its sharpness to the other side.

The world stayed still and sure. She could still feel the night breeze tickling along her skin. There were no voices calling her, no terror pushing her feet.

A bird began a song like a heartbeat somewhere over-head. The air smelt of gum leaves and cooling rocks and water. Barbara opened her eyes.

The world was sweet and cool. Barbara felt a smile spread until it seemed to stretch her toes. She was still in the gully. Somewhere above her Ma was cooking dinner and the O'Reillys were waiting, with love and laughter, around the shanty that was home. Barbara stood up and slowly filled the kero tin with water, then began the climb back. The last of the sunlight shone bright red through the branches and turned the tree trunks into fire.

'Tell me a story, Bubba.'

The fire flickered in the growing dark, licking like a small red animal at the thick dry branches Young Jim had dragged up the hill. Barbara looked down at the little girl in surprise.

'I'm not much good at stories,' she admitted.

'Yes you are.' Thellie climbed determinedly onto her knee and wriggled to get comfortable. Her bones felt sharp and light. 'Tell me a story like you told Young Jim. You know, about round the corner.'

Barbara looked at the small girl's trusting face, then glanced around. No-one else seemed to be listening. Ma was crocheting long strips of rag into a rug by the light of the newly lit lantern. Young Jim sat next to her, carving a bit of driftwood with his pocket-knife. Dad and Elaine had taken the other little ones down to the creek to wash the plates with sand and ashes in the last of the light. They still weren't back.

'Tell me what it's like round the corner,' Thellie urged again, folding her thin arms around Barbara's waist. It felt funny to have a kid on your lap, thought Barbara, but nice.

'All right,' she said slowly. She thought for a while. 'I don't know where to start,' she said finally.

Thellie wriggled impatiently. 'Tell me where people

live,' she ordered. 'Have they got palaces and white horses and crowns and songs and jewelled slippers?'

Barbara smiled. 'No, nothing like that.' She tried to think of something that would impress a small girl. 'We've got aeroplanes.'

'I've seen a hairyplane,' said Thellie scornfully. 'Last time we were up in town, there was one buzzed round the showground. You could see the pilot and everything. That's not from round the corner.'

'Not little planes. These are big planes.'

'How big?'

'Bigger than ... bigger than six houses. Big enough for hundreds of people.'

Thellie wriggled once again, satisfied. 'Did you ever go in one?'

'Once, when I was younger. I went up to Surfer's Paradise for a holiday. That's at the beach.'

'Did you stay in a palace?'

'Well, sort of. We stayed in a really tall building, twenty stories high, higher than ... than ... the gum trees, nearly as high as that ridge. There was a swimming pool right on the top so you could look out over the ocean and all the other buildings, and see the people like tiny beetles on the sand.'

Thellie giggled. 'Go on.'

Barbara racked her brains. 'And we've got machines that show you stories, just like you're really there.'

'Like the talking pictures.'

'Yeah, that's right, except nearly everyone's got one. It's called television — we say TV, for short. Some TVs are so small you can put them in your pocket and carry them around and look at them whenever you like. We've all got phones too, so you can ring anyone up when you feel like it.'

'Everyone?' asked Thellie.

'Nearly everyone. Young Jim could've rung you up to say he was coming home. And there's machines that do all your adding up for you, called calculators. You can fit them in your pocket, too, and there's computers, they ...' She couldn't think how to describe computers. 'They sort of think for you, and you can play games with them and they tell you if you've lost.'

Thellie wriggled, bored with the computers. Barbara wracked her brains. 'There's ... there's rocket ships.'

'What's a rocket ship?' demanded Thellie, scratching a mosquito bite on her ankle.

'Rocket ships take you to the moon.'

Thellie giggled, 'Did you ever go to the moon? Did you eat green cheese?'

'Green cheese?'

'Yes. The moon's made of green cheese.'

'No, it isn't. I've never been there, but other people have, oh, ages ago, before I was born. They said it's all dust that you sink into, and the gravity's so low you can jump as high as a gum tree without even trying and float down no matter how big you are. And there's no air on the moon so you have to wear this big suit to protect you.'

Suddenly, Barbara noticed the faces of Ma and Young Jim staring from the lamp light, Dad and Elaine and the little ones in the shadows, all listening to her words.

'Go on,' said Dad quietly. 'Tell us some more.'

'I, um, what do you want to know?'

'In this world around the corner,' said Dad softly, 'do all men have jobs? Are there susso camps in this fine world of yours?'

'There's unemployment,' said Barbara, trying to think. 'But it's not like this, not so many people out of work. I don't think there's any susso camps. Not that I've heard of anyway.'

'And everyone's got houses, proper houses, not shacks like this, and those TV things you mentioned?'

Barbara nodded. 'Mostly.'

'And are there doctors if you need them, and the kiddies go to school, all of them, not stuck away forgotten in a place like this, with no future in front of them, nothing for them, nothing ...'

'Dad!' Ma grabbed his shoulders. 'Don't you scare the girl. I won't have you speaking like that, you hear me? You've done your best for us. At least we've got a roof over our heads and full bellies. There's plenty worse off than us.'

Dad shook her off, still looking at Barbara. 'It's a poor comedown you're at then, isn't it? Down here with the likes of us. I don't know what Young Jim said he was taking you to, but I reckon you didn't count on this.'

Dad waved his bony hand at the flickering lantern, the clay-daubed shack, the makeshift chairs and table. His scar flickered pink and red. 'I reckon you wish you were back in your nice soft bed with school tomorrow and—'

'Dad, don't! Leave her alone!' It was Young Jim's voice, somewhere in the dimness, but it didn't matter, her voice seemed to come all by itself. Thellie slid down her legs as she rose.

'It wasn't like that! It wasn't!' She was shaking. It

seemed like her voice wasn't hers. She didn't want to ... it couldn't be her. 'It was horrible. Horrible. I was living with Aunt Ellie, but she wasn't my aunt, not really, it was just a foster home, then she got sick and I had to go back to Mum. Mum said she was off the drugs, she promised she was, she promised. But the first morning I found the syringe in the bathroom and I asked her, "Are you on smack again, are you?", and she just laughed, and her friend laughed too. He was a new friend and he was horrible. He said things to me, horrible things. I was scared and I ran, but I didn't know where to go. I slept that night in a used clothes bin for St Vinnie's, but there were rats, then I found these kids, they were older than me, but they said they were on the streets too and I could stay with them and they were going to this demonstration. I didn't know what it was about, but ...'

She couldn't say anything more. She didn't have to. Dad's arm was around her shoulder and Ma was on the other side. Young Jim was patting her back and Elaine and the little ones were crying. Dad was muttering something that sounded like, 'I'm sorry Bubba love, I'm sorry,' and Ma was telling her that it was all right, everything was fine, and then Elaine trod on someone's foot.

'It's like a blooming football scrum,' complained Young Jim. Then Barbara laughed and everyone else started giggling. Dad gave her a final hug, then stepped back and looked at her, his face in shadow with the lantern light behind him.

'But you went around that corner of yours, and came here,' he finished for her.

'And a good thing too,' said Ma. 'If I had my way I'd hang people who scare kids up with the washing and watch them wave in the breeze.'

Barbara sat down again, her knees suddenly shaky. Thellie clambered onto her lap again and wound her arms around her neck. She held the small girl tightly.

'It's better here,' Barbara said finally. 'I'm not scared. I know it's just a shack, but it's like you've everything here you need.'

Dad began to laugh, the bitterness creeping back into his voice. 'A dirt floor and dole rations once a week, with weevils in the flour and bush rats at the soap.' The laugh broke off.

'We do all right,' said Ma quietly. 'We manage.'

Dad looked at her queerly. 'It's you who manage,' he said softly. 'Me, I'm good for nothing now.'

'And I won't hear you talk like that,' Ma went on, with a touch of desperation. 'You've done your best for us, you break your back for us. This place isn't so bad. When I think of the poor souls in those other camps, places like Happy Valley, with everyone bickering and sniping and cockroaches big as mice and rats as big as footballs and all the kids with the runs, I know that at least we've got neighbours we can depend on here in the gully. We'll see it through.'

Ma bent down, picked up her crocheting from the leaves and bark where it had fallen and piled it on the table. 'Come on,' she said softly. 'It's time you lot were all in bed. Bubba too. You'll feel better in the morning, love. You'll have forgotten all about it after a good night's sleep.' It was as though she was trying to convince herself.

It was dark inside the shack. The lantern gave too little light to penetrate the cracks. Barbara could hear the steady breathing of the little ones, Elaine sort of muttering in her sleep, Young Jim's quiet snore.

Ma and Dad were speaking in low voices outside.

'What do you reckon?' It was Dad's voice.

There was a pause. Barbara could almost see Ma's fingers leaping with the crochet hook, as though it helped her think.

'I don't know,' she said finally. 'It sounded so real. I'd say it's the truth. Or what she thinks is the truth anyway.'

'You don't think it was a bump on the head, like Young Jim said?'

'She couldn't have made all that up,' said Ma. 'Not in so much detail. It seemed so real.'

'A world around the corner,' said Dad slowly. 'Imagine it! What a world I'd take you to then. What sort of world would you have love, if you could choose?'

There was a silence.

Then Barbara heard Ma's quiet voice. 'I don't think I've got the energy left to dream,' she was saying. 'I just try to be thankful for what we've got and make the best of it. I think maybe I'm frightened to dream, in case I can't keep smiling when I wake up.'

There was another silence.

'I'm sorry love. For bringing you here. For failing you all.' There was a stifled sob. Someone moved quickly.

'Ah, I'm sorry, love,' said Dad's voice again. 'I didn't mean to make you cry.'

'Can't you see?' Ma's voice was different. Not the calm strong voice Barbara had heard before. 'I can stand anything, but not you like this. You haven't failed us. It's not your fault. It's not! Can't you see?'

There was a longer silence. The first rays of moonlight sifted through the cracks in the wall, bright as torchlight, golden as Gully Jack's dreams. Then Dad's voice, very quiet. 'Somewhere around the corner,' he said. 'I wonder.'

DULCIE OF THE DAIRY FARM

On Wednesdays, the single men came down the valley to get their dole rations. On Thursdays, the family men came, by themselves if they had to come a long way or with their wives and children, the kids with bare feet and the women with tired eyes. It was a long walk from Poverty Gully down to the main arm of the valley where Sergeant Ryan presided at the police station, handing out the tickets that allowed you to get your dole rations at Nicholson's store — so much tea, flour and sugar, golden syrup, soap and matches and a bit of cheese.

It was usually the same faces, week after week. The farms were too small to lure others to the valley with dreams of a bit of work. No-one thought there was still gold in the creek either, except Gully Jack, thought Dulcie. She sighed a little, thinking of Gully Jack.

Thursday mornings began early at Dulcie's. The kindling had to be brought in to light the fire so the bread could be cooked for breakfast, the cows had to be milked at first light, half-asleep bodies warm and furry where you leant your head against them, flicking manure-sodden tails at you so you had to wash as soon as you came in, the smell of them lingering in your hair all day. The pigs would run squealing through the mud to feed on the small potatoes Dulcie had cooked in milk. The cream had to be left to rise in the stone dairy where the floor was wet with cold and moss grew in the corners when she didn't have the time to scrub it out.

Sometimes Dulcie thought her whole life had been cows. The low moan of cows waiting for milking was behind her every memory — every time she thought of her mother she heard the song of the cows, or smelt their warm teats and warmer milk on her fingers.

All her childhood had been cows, except for the years when she boarded during the week up in town to 'get her learning'. Cows to milk on hot summer afternoons, while the flies bumped at the bucket and tried to sip the cream. Cows to milk on frosty mornings when the white grass bit your toes and the only relief from chilblains was to find a fresh hot cow pat, still steaming on the grass, and warm your toes in it.

It had been easier when her father was alive, thought Dulcie, and not just because the butter prices were better then. Four hands to do the work, not just hers, getting harder and redder around the knuckles and more cracked each year. But Johnny Bill was working for his board and keep now there was no money to pay him — not with butter prices the way they were, not with floods and drought and cows that kept on getting sick so you never knew what lay around the next corner. If her brothers had come back from the war it might have been different, but they hadn't, and there it was; what couldn't be cured must be endured. At times she thought her bones would break, they ached so much. But you had to keep on going. There was so much to do, so many people who needed so much.

After the milking there was breakfast to be eaten on the hop, a slice of bread with a soft-boiled egg spread on it, eaten from one hand as she picked vegies, still sweet from the dew, out of the garden, and then the bacon to be chopped and thrown in the copper to make soup for the susso families later in the day. Potatoes from last autumn, soft and just on sprouting in the big sacks in the pantry, carrots, turnips, parsnips, cabbage, tomatoes in the summer, or peas in winter, and onions that made her cry. Johnny Bill would light the fire underneath the copper to cook the soup, the same as he lit it on Mondays so she could do the washing.

Soup didn't cost you anything if you grew it all yourself; the vegies fed with cow manure, the bacon from the pigs that Johnny Bill slaughtered for her every autumn which they smoked over the meat-house fire, half for her and half for Johnny Bill as payment for the extra work.

You could feed an army with soup, the copper keeping it hot and bubbling, like the creek below the falls, and by lunch it was ready to hand over the gate to anyone who passed. For kids there was the buttermilk, left over after the milk had been churned to butter, as much as they could drink, kept in big iron buckets, while the women rested on the verandah.

It was a good life, thought Dulcie, if only she weren't so tired; if only her hands didn't ache with cold sometimes; if only the kitchen wasn't so empty-feeling at night, so that you were glad you were so tired, and didn't have the energy to think about how lonely you felt. You didn't even have the energy to dream at night of what things *might* be like.

Dulcie glanced at the sketch that hung on the wall, roughly framed with sanded wood. Johnny Bill had done the framing. But who had drawn the sketch she couldn't say. It was a drawing of her house, but as it might be, with a new solid verandah; with a garden at the front and tidy fruit trees growing in nice neat lines. There was a child's swing hanging from one tree and you could almost hear the laughter of other kids, somewhere around the corner.

Dulcie forced herself to look away. The drawing had been propped on her front doormat last birthday. No-one remembered when her birthday was nowadays. Perhaps Gully Jack remembered, but he hadn't put a pencil in his hand since he left school. Who except Gully Jack could dream like that, could see new life in her old house, could see the children that came when she was dreaming ... Dulcie gave herself a shake. Dreaming got you nowhere fast. It was time to get on with the soup.

Dulcie had been serving soup on Thursdays for two years now, since the first susso families moved down to the gully, hoping for gold and disappointed. They stayed, lulled by the peace of the valley, or just because there was nowhere left to go. They were grateful, mostly, though a few took it for granted and complained about the carrots or the lack of dumplings, but those were the bad sorts, grumblers and no-hopers, who Sergeant Ryan quietly suggested should move on. Some of them were embarrassed, generally the men, at having to eat charity. They sat sipping quietly without meeting your eyes, and left as quietly. Others, like Dad O'Reilly, tried to do what they could in return, by chopping wood or mending fences. Her fences hadn't been as taut since her dad was alive.

There was one man, it was more than a year ago now. There was something wrong with his leg, because he walked with a crutch. When he took his soup she saw that there were only two fingers on one hand. He was one of those who drank without looking at you, his mouth twisted with more than bitterness, so she wondered if his leg or his hand still hurt. But when he'd finished he hadn't slipped away. He unrolled his swag; first the bit of sacking, then the blanket, then an old jacket worn at the seams. They'd been protecting a banjo. He cradled it above his lap and played it, in spite of his lost fingers; songs and reels that jiggled across the verandah until you thought the magpies would be dancing, and she knew he was paying her for the soup. If he couldn't chop wood he would play.

He played until the soup was finished, until the shadows were thickening and she'd gone inside, to wash up, and only the last of the men were leaning against the verandah posts as the dew began to wet the grass. His voice changed then. It grew harsher, lower, as though it was a song he didn't want her to hear.

'I went off to fight for my country,

I went off far over the sea,

I went off to fight for my country,

And this is what it gave to me.

Soup, soup,

They gave me a big bowl of loop the loop,

Soup, soup,

They gave me a big bowl of soup ...'

The voices of the other ragged, grim-faced susso men joined in, and she wondered how many of them had fought in the war, how many had been wounded or shell-shocked, how many had come home to a life of poverty, or susso camps, or desperation.

The song died away. She took her hands out of the bowl of greasy water and stepped out onto the verandah, but the singers had gone. There was no sign of the man with the banjo.

He didn't come the next week, or the next. She asked Sergeant Ryan, but he hadn't seen him. He must have moved on, like most of the single men, humping their swag to a new place every week to look for work and collect their dole. But who would hire him, lame in hand and leg? It hurt to think of the miles he must have come, and the miles he still had to go.

He might have been her brothers, or any of the blokes she'd gone to school with, the brave bright blokes who'd ridden off so happily to their graves in France or Turkey. Sometimes it seemed to her the war was simply resting, jealously guarding the men it had taken, waiting until it could feed again.

She'd done her best to make a difference, not just with soup. It was habit in the valley now for anyone with anything to spare to leave it at Dulcie's — baby clothes or blankets or tin that could be hammered for shanty roofs, hessian sacks or battered saucepans. She'd badgered nearly everyone in the valley to give what they could. But it was a long way to bring even a blanket, back up the valley to the gully, when you had a week's dole rations on your back as well.

Dulcie cajoled Sergeant Ryan into ferrying things up in the police car, dole rations too, for those who found the walk too hard. It was against regulations, Sergeant Ryan complained, but Dulcie told him, nonsense, it was his duty to keep law and order wasn't it, and to check that all parts of the district remained peaceful? That's all he was doing on his trips up to the gully, keeping the place peaceful, and if it just so happened there were a few bundles in the back, or a dance on up at the hall ...

He'd help her cart whatever was needed. He'd call by for a cup of tea and a chat about who needed what, and where, and he'd sit with her in church. Sometimes she dreamed he might ask her to a dance, the one down in the gully, or one in town. But he never had.

Sometimes it seemed he didn't have a life except his duty. He was a good man, Sergeant Ryan, thought Dulcie as she sliced the last of the cabbage into the soup. He was kind and he cared, even if he didn't have dreams like Gully Jack, but then, dreams got in the way of real life at times. You had to pick and choose your dreams.

The first of the sussos were coming down the road.

There were the O'Reilly kids, pulling out grass, lush and green from gutter water, for the cows and poking it through the fence to tempt them.

Stupid cows, thought Dulcie tolerantly, the grass was as sweet in their own paddock, especially down near the creek. But maybe they liked the company. Cows gave more milk if you talked to them, Dulcie knew that for sure. Maybe they liked the chatter of the kids as well.

There was a new kid with them this morning — a strange-looking kid with shortish hair. Maybe she'd been sick, thought Dulcie. She was thin enough. She needed feeding up, like all the kids she saw.

'Hoy! You lot! Up here!' Dulcie yelled through the window.

The kids gave the cows one last scratch behind the horns and tossed the last of the grass over the fence for the cows to nose at, and raced up the path to the verandah, bare feet thudding on the old stone path.

'Hey, Dulcie, Gully Jack's nearly finished his new channel, it's right up near the bend.'

'Hey, Dulcie, the new Friesian's got a calf, it's mostly black. Did you know?'

'Of course she knows, you dingbat, they're her cows aren't they? Hey, Dulcie, did you see—'

'Dulcie, this is Bubba. Bubba, this is Dulcie. She's got the best cows in New South Wales. Hey, Dulcie, do you think the new calf—'

Dulcie broke through the chatter and took Barbara's hand.

'Pleased to meet you, Bubba.'

'My name's Barbara, really.' The way she spoke was different from the others. Dulcie looked at her curiously.

'Are you related to the O'Reillys?' she asked.

The girl shook her head. 'No—'

'Yes, you are,' interrupted Elaine. 'Ma said you were, so there. You're one of us now. You're Bubba O'Reilly.'

Dulcie grinned. Trust Ma O'Reilly to take in a stray. She liked Ma O'Reilly. They were cut from the same cloth. And Dad O'Reilly was a good sort, or he might be if things were different, if he just had something he could hope for.

'All right then, you're an O'Reilly now. What were you before, if I may ask?'

'She won't tell us!'

'I have told you.' The girl's voice was quiet. Her face had lost the laughter that shone while she'd been feeding the cows.

'You haven't told us your last name yet,' insisted Elaine.

'You just shut up,' Young Jim hissed.

'All you've told us is you come from—'

'Somewhere round the corner,' chorused Thellie and Joey, as though it was something wonderful.

Dulcie looked at Barbara. She was trying to smile too, but couldn't. It was as though it was still all too new. Young Jim put his arm around her shoulders and glared at the others. Dulcie clucked her tongue. 'Well, who's going to give me a hand this morning?'

'Me me me!' the young kids clamoured.

'Well, you lot, I want you to get the eggs. All of them, mind, no missing the ones in the shed or you won't be getting any to take home, and the old black chook is laying in the brambles by the creek so don't miss that nest either. Elaine and Jim, can you go and pick some apples for me from the old tree just across the creek? Grandpa's seedling with the red and yellow stripes. None of the other trees have ripe fruit yet. You'll find some boxes in the shed.' Dulcie paused to find a breath. 'Bubba, you come and help me get the scones out of the oven, they'll be burning if I leave them in another minute.'

'I'm staying with Bubba,' said Young Jim.

Dulcie glanced at him. His chin was jutting out, just like his Dad's. Dulcie smothered a grin. He looked like he thought she was going to tie the girl to a kitchen chair and try and beat the information out of her, instead of feeding her scones and asking — just asking — a few questions. After all, it was neighbourly to be curious. How could you help people if you didn't know all there was to know?

'Come on then Barbara, and Jim too, if that's what you want. Those scones'll be charcoal soon.'

It was hot in the kitchen. The walls had taken the heat from the stove and breathed it back. The flies dozed at the window, too hot even to buzz as far as the washhouse to smell the soup. Dulcie took the trays of hot scones out of the oven.

'Here,' she said to Young Jim, 'you start spreading these out to cool, and then you can start buttering that lot over there. And mind you don't stint the jam either. It's last year's apple jelly and it'll go off if I don't use it soon.'

'What can I do?' asked Barbara.

'You can start eating scones, that's what you can do,' ordered Dulcie. 'Look at you, so thin your smile'd fall off you if it wasn't glued on. There, that's better. I like to see a smile. You get that lot inside you.'

'What about Jim?' asked Barbara.

'He knows he doesn't have to ask. Look at him now.' Young Jim grinned through a mouthful of scone.

'But you make sure you get those buttered just the same.' Dulcie scooped more flour into her old brown mixing bowl and poured in buttermilk and began to mix the dough. 'I want to get six more trays done by lunchtime.'

'D'you need any wood split, Dulcie?' asked Young Jim, finishing off his scone.

Dulcie shook her head. 'Johnny Bill split some for me

yesterday, but thanks all the same. Maybe next week you can split me a big pile. But if you do, I'm paying you for it, mind.'

'No,' said Young Jim. 'I'm not taking your money, Dulcie. Ma would skin me alive, and she'd be right too.'

'Then I'll pay you in eggs,' said Dulcie mildly. 'No-one said anything about money, did they?'

The flies buzzed drowsily at the window. The hot air shivered above the metal stove.

Barbara finished her second scone and began to dab at the jam smears on her plate. She glanced up at Dulcie. Dulcie was watching her curiously, like a sparrow hoping for crumbs. She didn't say anything, but Barbara could feel her curiosity, thick as the scone dough sticking between her fingers.

It seemed mean not to tell her, when she was so generous and so badly wanted to know.

'I'll tell you where I came from if you like,' said Barbara slowly. 'I've told the O'Reillys. I think they sort of believe me. But you'll think it's crazy.'

'Try me,' said Dulcie, patting at the dough. 'I'd believe anything, I would. If you told me butter was green I'd probably believe you. I mean it's made from grass, isn't it? The grass feeds the cows and the cows make the butter.' She smiled delightedly at Barbara's laugh.

'There, I knew you could laugh if you wanted to. You tell me where you came from and I promise I'll believe you.'

'Bubba,' said Young Jim warningly.

Barbara looked at him and shrugged.

'I think I'm from the future,' she said hesitantly. She

glanced at Dulcie. Dulcie's hands had risen from the scone dough. They rested, all white and sticky, on the bowl, but she didn't say anything.

Barbara went on: 'It happened so suddenly. It's still so hard to realise it happened at all. I was scared. And this old guy told me if you're frightened you just go around the corner, so I did. I don't know how to explain it. I was scared and I just imagined around the corner and then I was somewhere else, but still in Sydney, and it was an unemployed workers demonstration and Jim was there and he dragged me away.'

Dulcie found her voice.

'From the demonstration?' she asked.

'Yes. I didn't have anywhere to go, so I came with Jim.'

Dulcie dropped her hands back into the bowl. She began to roll the dough out, patting it into scone shapes and flouring them before she dropped them on the tray.

'And what about your home?'

'I don't have a home,' said Barbara.

'But your parents! Won't they be worried?'

'No,' said Barbara.

'Are you an orphan then? Heavens girl, everyone has a home somewhere.'

'I don't,' said Barbara.

'Yes, you do. Your home's with us.' Young Jim's voice was firm.

Barbara's smile was tentative. 'All right,' she said. 'Maybe I do have a home.'

Dulcie looked at them, half shaken, half reassured. She reached into the cool safe to pour them mugs of buttermilk. When people are in trouble, feed them up, was Dulcie's motto, and she supposed the girl was in trouble; or maybe she was out of it, maybe she was free and home, after all.

Somewhere around the corner. She could think of a lot of people who'd like a new world around the corner. 'This going around the corner bit. Can anyone do it, do you think?'

'I don't know,' said Barbara shyly. 'The old guy that told me, he said it hadn't worked for him. Maybe you have to be really scared, like I was, and there were hands, too, like someone was helping me around. But the old man said he'd known someone who'd done it, just like me.'

'It's a good thing to think of, though,' said Dulcie dreamily. 'A new world just around the corner, a good world, where things are better than this.' She shrugged and began pinching out the scones. 'But I don't suppose there is, at least not for most of us. We've just got to be content with what we've got.'

Young Jim ate another scone absently.

'I think ... there's another world,' he said, slowly. 'Sometimes I can see it, just like Bubba's — it's so close, just like she said, almost like it's round the corner. But I reckon I can't just fly there or whatever she did. I reckon I've got to work for it. You've got to change this world to get to the new one.'

There were yells from the back gate and the young kids burst in with the eggs, then Elaine came in hefting a giant box of apples and the kitchen was filled with crumbs and shouts and laughter again — even Bubba was laughing — and they all ran out again to see the calf, though they'd be back at lunchtime, thought Dulcie, for soup with their

Dad, when he came back with the rations from the store.

Dulcie put some apples in a basket and took it out to the verandah. Anyone could help themselves to them, there were apples enough to spare. She looked over to the kids again, at Bubba with her short and shining hair, at Young Jim hovering at her side.

Somewhere around the corner ... Dulcie's eyes were far away. Where would she go, she wondered suddenly, if she could travel around the corner. She had all she loved right here — the farm, the valley, the cows. Gully Jack's face flashed by her eyes, a dreaming face, laughing as he lifted small gold specks up to the sun.

A child's laughter broke through her dream. That's what she'd have, she realised, if she could travel around a corner. Kids of her own, to feed and cuddle and look after, but there was no way Gully Jack could fit into that dream. He was happy with his house falling down around his ears, with his gullies and obsessions. You needed a solid man if you wanted kids, a dependable man like Ted Ryan ... Theophilous Arnold Ryan ... if only he had dreams as well. How could you live with a man who had no dreams? What would your kids be like if their father had no dreams?

Dulcie watched the O'Reilly children out the window as she split more scones and dabbed on the butter. Good rich butter it was too, though a bit too white to sell well. You didn't get the colour here, from the summer pasture.

The valley was so far from a good market anyway. That girl, Bubba, was stretching out her fingers to stroke the calf, like she'd never touched a cow before, and the other kids were around her, egging her on, encouraging her, protecting her. She'd be all right now, Dulcie told herself, whatever she'd been through. The O'Reillys would look after her. Dulcie glanced out the window again.

She just wished she could be sure.

NICHOLSON'S STORE

Nicholson's store smelt of prunes and sacks of bran and the broken biscuits he kept by the counter and sold at so much for a penny; it smelt of the cheese, hot and sweating, that sat under the glass on the counter, where Mr Nicholson presided in his starched white apron, taking the dole tickets with a face as bitter as his own molasses and handing out rations in exchange. It was only sussos in the store on Thursday. The valley people got their groceries on other days. Nicholson looked like he'd be happy to sweep the sussos out with the worn broom he kept behind the door, but he took their tickets anyway, for the money he got when he sent them in.

Young Jim glanced in at the queue in front of the counter. They were gully people, familiar faces, embarrassed men or harassed women, and men who looked belligerent or defiant, as though daring old Nicholson to say a word. Strangers in the valley were often single men, just passing through, hoping for work or filling up their lives with travel if they couldn't. They would have got their rations the day before.

'No sign of Dad yet,' said Young Jim. 'He must still be

up at the police station.' He sidled in the front door of the shop and edged along the sacks of oats.

'Where are you going?' whispered Barbara. Mr Nicholson looked too intimidating to speak out aloud.

Young Jim gestured towards the far end of the counter, where a pile of newspapers was hidden from Mr Nicholson behind the tins of biscuits. 'I want to have a dekko at the paper, that's all. See if there's anything in it about the demonstration. Hey, imagine if we'd got our photo in the paper!'

Barbara followed him. Thellie and Joey looked bored and ran out into the sunlight again. They sat on the verandah wriggling their feet in the dust and watching the people pass.

'Hey, look here!' said Young Jim.

'Is it something about the demonstration?'

'Nah, I suppose it was too small for them to bother, evictions are two a penny nowadays. No, listen to this, it's a letter. It's real good.' He began to read:

'Dear Sir,

Optimism and sturdy independence are the chief characteristics of the Australian race. Australians are not easily daunted — a fact proven countless times in peace and war throughout the British Empire — and their spirit of independence goes almost beyond a virtue. Many men made provision for a rainy day, but the economic storm which has seized the world in its grip has exhausted all that they have saved. The decent man finds idleness irksome. At a meeting of the Advisory Council—'

'He's on his soapbox again.' Elaine came up behind them. 'Who wants to hear that stuff? Turn the page over so I can read the serial. Go on, be a sport, it's getting exciting — there was this girl, see, her name's Isabel, and she met this man but it turns out he was on leave and had to go back to East Africa and—'

Young Jim snorted. 'Soppy stuff. Hey, look at this, it's about an exploding cow.'

Barbara looked over his shoulder. The paper looked strange, with small print and narrow columns, headed *Political*, *Telegraph* and *Pastoral News*. The ads were the brightest spots in the paper; old-fashioned looking drawings with big headlines:

Why Keep Hens and Buy Eggs? You won't have to if Karswood's part of their diet.

Karswood's blood enriching tonic ...

On a motor cycle at 76 — there's life in the old dog yet, with Kruschen's salts.

Kruschen's for constipation ...

I got from 1 egg to 8 eggs a day with Karswood blood enriching tonic ...

Wood's great Peppermint cure for Colds and Influenza ...

His boss knows best! All over the British Empire they take Kruschen's for

constipation!

Carg and Mostyn, buyers for wattle bark and rabbit skins ...

Kruschen's keeps constipation at bay ...

Young Jim was still reading.

' *"While a cow belonging to a farmer at Harold's Creek was contentedly chewing her cud the other day, she suddenly exploded with a roar and fragments of her head were found all over the district"*.

'Hey, how come nothing like this ever happens to us?' complained Young Jim.

''Cause we don't have a cow, silly,' Elaine informed him.

'Nah to you too.

"Evidently the unfortunate animal had been grazing near a box of detonators—"'

A hand came down suddenly across the counter. It was white and hairy with a faint smell of old cheese. It grabbed the paper out of Young Jim's hand and pushed him roughly away.

'What do you lot think you're doing, eh? Blooming susso kids. This isn't a penny library. If you want to read the paper you can pay for it.'

Barbara looked up at the shopkeeper's face. Why was he so angry? He looked back at her, his small eyes green in his red face. 'What are you staring at, missy? I don't want your sort cluttering up my shop. Those papers are tuppence each. If you haven't got money to spend you can get on out of it.'

Young Jim stepped in front of her. 'We have got money to spend,' he said coolly. He drew Sergeant Ryan's sixpence out of his pocket. 'I'd like five musk sticks and five cobbers, and let's see, how much are the gobstoppers?' he asked Mr Nicholson politely. 'If you don't mind, we really are in a hurry.'

Elaine giggled. 'Come on, let's leave him to it,' she whispered. She drew a deep breath as they emerged out on the verandah. 'Old Nicholson's store always seems stuffy. Don't know why. Other shops smell so good. Must be him, I suppose, or maybe he's got mice.'

Young Jim came out after them, holding a small white paper bag. He handed each of them a tall pink stick and a pale green lolly, as big as a small hen's egg, thought Barbara. She looked at hers doubtfully.

'What is it?'

'A gobstopper. Don't you know gobstoppers? They'll last all day if you suck slowly. They turn different colours too. Just remember to take it out and stick it in your pocket when you go to Dulcie's for lunch.' Elaine popped hers in her mouth. 'Droubble is yo cand dalk broberly wid dem in yer mouf.'

Young Jim laughed. 'I'll keep mine for later,' he said. 'I'm going up to see how Dad's doing at the station and maybe thank Sergeant Ryan again. You coming?'

Elaine shook her head. 'I'll dake Dellie and Doey down do loog ad de gows adain,' she said. 'Dee oo.' She took Thellie's and Joey's hands and they wandered back up the road towards the dairy farm. Barbara and Young Jim began to walk past the pub and the butcher's, towards the police station.

'Does it take long to get a dole ticket?' asked Barbara.

Young Jim shrugged. 'Can take hours. It's not so bad now — most of the blokes who came here at the start have moved on again. It's a real cow for Sergeant Ryan to get through everyone. It takes him most of Wednesday and Thursday every week. Sergeant Ryan's real good about it though. Some coppers search you to make sure you haven't got any money on you before they give you your ticket. Sergeant Ryan wouldn't do a thing like that. He *can* be tough — you don't find any smart alecs trying to get the dole twice here.' He shook his head. 'It makes me so mad when stuck-up whingers like old Nicholson complain about the dole. What would old Nicholson know about going hungry, or losing your job?'

'Soapbox,' suggested Barbara.

Young Jim chuckled. 'All right,' he said. 'I know I go

on a bit. You just shut me up, Bubba. Hey, what did you think of Dulcie? She's a bit of all right, isn't she? She'd do anything for anyone, Dulcie would.'

'I liked her,' said Barbara slowly.

She wondered if she should mention the touch of sadness, the hint of loneliness in Dulcie's eyes. Was that why she helped other people, to lessen the loneliness inside? She shook her head. If Dulcie was lonely it was none of her business.

Young Jim took a deep breath. 'Smells good, doesn't it,' he said. 'I don't believe there's air anywhere in the world like the valley — cow pats and dry grass and trees and all. You don't know what you're smelling half the time in Sydney, and when you do you don't like it.'

They walked in silence for a while, the road dusty beneath their feet, the cattle curious on either side. The valley houses seemed perched among the paddocks, not crowded together like a town at all. Perhaps there'd been more houses once, thought Barbara, before the gold ran out. The road curved and narrowed into a bridge made of thick unpainted timber above a trickle of a creek choked with weed and watercress. A boy about her age dangled his legs off one side of the bridge. A bit of string like a fishing line dropped from his fingers into the thin snake of water.

The boy stared at them. He looked vaguely familiar.

'Pretend you don't see him,' muttered Young Jim out of the corner of his mouth.'

'Why?' whispered Barbara, but it was too late. They were on the bridge. Young Jim took Barbara's arm and hurried her along it. The boy didn't speak till they were off the bridge and onto the road again. Then they heard his voice behind them.

> 'Hallelujah I'm a bum,
> Hallelujah bum again,
> Hallelujah give us a handout,
> To revive us again.'

Barbara turned. The boy was gazing down at his fishing line, as though the song had nothing to do with Jim and Barbara at all. 'Who is he?'

'Nicholson's son, of course.' Young Jim's voice was grim. 'The lousy so-and-so knows I can't deck him one.'

'Why not?'

''Cause he's had scarlet fever and strained his heart. That's why he's not up in town at school. Come on, don't pay any attention. He'll stop soon if we pretend we can't hear.'

'What's scarlet fever?'

Young Jim stared at her. 'Don't tell me you don't get sick in your world? Scarlet fever's ... well ... you're sick, that's all, and you get a red rash. Kids can die of scarlet fever.'

'Can't they give them antibiotics or immunise them or something?'

'Immu — who?' Young Jim shook his head. 'Here, have another musk stick. Maybe it's lack of food.'

Barbara chewed the musk stick. It was as though the boy's song had made the strangeness of this world come alive again, as though only the comfort of the O'Reilly's, and Dulcie of course, and Gully Jack, was holding it back. 'Jim?'

'Mmmm.'

Jim was watching a falcon swoop into a nearby paddock. 'Hey, did you see that, Bubba?'

'Are you sure your parents won't change their minds? About me staying with you all I mean. They've got so many kids of their own already.'

'Of course they won't change their minds.' Jim's voice was scornful. 'They never changed their minds with me, did they?'

'What do you mean?'

'Ma and Dad aren't my real parents — I mean, they are now, but they weren't then. My parents were killed in a fire when I was just a nipper, about two I think. I can't really remember. Dad and Ma lived next door. They adopted me. They didn't have any kids of their own then, they'd just got married, and they looked after Sam and Edith for years. Their ma died and their father worked with Dad. They lived with us till he got married again. Ma cried for days after Sam and Edith left. I think Ma would look after the world if she could. Just like Dulcie.'

'Like you, a bit,' said Barbara.

'Like me? Cripes, I don't want to look after the world, I want to change it. I mean, it's just not right the way it is, is it? I mean—'

Barbara laughed. 'Soapbox,' she said again.

'Soapbox yourself.' Young Jim grabbed her hand. 'Come on, there's Dad. Let's run! The sooner we get to Dulcie's the sooner we get lunch. I'm starved!'

FRIDAY

Friday was bath morning. Dad and Young Jim lugged load after load of water in kero tins as soon as the fried tomatoes from breakfast were cleared away. They sweated up the hill from the creek until the creek was nearly dry, Dad said. Barbara and Elaine fed the fire with bits of twig and dry wood to keep it burning hot. The water steamed and bubbled on the coals, sending droplets of water snickering and whispering onto the hot ash where they bubbled and spluttered until they disappeared.

They washed the little ones first, giggling and wriggling and soapy in the old tin bath, and then they washed their clothes in the same water, pushing and scrubbing them until they were clean, then hanging them on the thornbushes to dry. Dad, careful not to lose a drop, poured the water on the tomatoes — the best drink they got all week — and the little ones ran naked in the sunlight, laughing and getting grubby feet and knees all over again.

'Let them run,' said Ma comfortably. 'A bit of sun on their hides won't do them any harm till their clothes are dry. Come on Young Jim, you fill it up again. I've been looking forward to this all week.'

Ma washed next, then Elaine. Then it was Barbara's

turn, cramped in the tin bath with the breeze on her shoulders and a kookaburra staring at her from the branch above, with only the thornbushes for privacy. No-one would peek, Elaine assured her, 'Because they knew if they did we'd peek at them, and anyway, Ma would give them what for if they tried.'

It was strange to bathe outside, with the sun on your skin and the curious ants running along the rim of the bath as though the water was ant soup that they could take away to store. The trees swayed overhead, their leaves bunched like soft green pillows. If only she could reach up and pull one down to rest her head on.

'Hey, come on slowcoach, it'll be half past lunchtime before we're finished at this rate!'

Barbara dressed in the clothes Ma had given her the day before. Ma had put her jeans away for Joey to wear when he got bigger. She wouldn't accept that they were fit for girls at all. 'And as for that thing you call a T-shirt, it's hardly decent. That world you come from may be all very well my girl, but you'd think someone'd think to dress a child properly. Look, there's this real nice skirt that Dulcie sent up last week. If I just take up the hem and give it a good airing you can put it on tonight.'

'That way it'll be clean for the dance,' Elaine explained. 'Everybody dresses up Friday night.' She leant over the fire and shook her wet hair. The water spat and hissed as it landed on the coals.

Young Jim looked up. He was carving something by the fire, scraping at the wood with his pocketknife so the shavings fell in little curls over his knees. Barbara bent over to look.

'What is it?'

'A brooch for Ma. She can wear it tonight if she wants. See, it's a flower. I reckon if I thread a bit of wire back here—'

'It's lovely,' said Barbara.

Young Jim grinned. 'I'll make you one for next week if you like. Hey, what are we going to do now?'

'Nothing,' decided Elaine. 'I'm staying clean for tonight.'

'Let's go get some eels,' suggested Young Jim. 'Hey Ma, you'd like some eels, wouldn't you?'

'Urk. Nasty slimy things,' protested Elaine. 'We'll get mud all over us.'

'Well, you don't have to touch them. You can just play Lady Muck and watch us catch them. You coming, kids?'

'No, they're not,' said Ma firmly. 'You lot can go if you want. At least you can wash yourselves after. I'm not cleaning this lot again before tonight. You can take your lunch with you. Two slices each and mind you don't cut them too wide, that bread's got to last till tomorrow lunch because I'm not making any scones till then, and will someone please eat that tomato jam — it's going to go to waste if you don't.'

'We'll eat it Ma,' said Young Jim soothingly. 'You going to come, Elaine, or not?'

'I suppose.' Elaine uncurled herself and stretched. 'But I'm not touching any eels, mind. And I'm not carrying them either.'

Young Jim hunted around for string and bits of meat from the night before.

'That's how you catch eels,' he explained to Barbara, as

they started down the track. 'They grab hold of the meat and won't let go. Then you just haul them onto the bank.'

'That's when the real fun starts,' agreed Elaine. 'These great slimy things wriggling all over the place trying to get back into the water and biting if you get anywhere near them.'

'Garn, they aren't that bad,' protested Young Jim.

'They're worse,' said Elaine decidedly, pushing a branch out of her way. The track was filled with midday shadows; short and fat, thick with gum leaf scent and dancing sunlight and the faint tang of smoke from hot dry wood.

'I reckon everyone in the gully's having a wash,' said Young Jim. 'I bet shirts and skirts are hanging on every bush.' He kicked at a rock. 'Makes you mad, doesn't it? I mean, I bet up in Sydney there are rich people with marble bathrooms and gold taps and ... and everything. Down here people like Ma and the Hendersons don't even have a bath they can fit their knees in.'

'I liked bathing in the sunlight,' said Barbara dreamily. 'It was like having someone pour warm smoke down your back. I bet my skin's gold if I could see.'

Young Jim pulled back the neck of her blouse and peered down her back. 'Nah,' he said, 'still the same colour. Pink and lots of freckles.'

Barbara tried to kick him. He dodged, laughing. 'Nah,' he went on seriously. 'That's not the point anyway. I mean, I don't mind having a bath under the gum trees. Cripes, I reckon it's better than a marble bathroom any day. I mean rich people can bathe in the sun or bathe inside. We don't get to choose.'

'I'd choose sunlight any day,' said Barbara.

Elaine snorted. 'That's all very well when it's sunny,' she informed them. 'How about in winter and your knees freeze because you can't fit them in the tub?'

'See, that's what I mean,' said Young Jim.

'Well, you go and get your soapbox and tell everyone then,' said Elaine tranquilly. 'Not us. We've heard it all before.' She thrust her hands through her wet hair again, untangling the rat's tails as it dried in the sun.

The eel pool was down near the main road, where the creek slowed down to a more sedate pace after bubbling down the gully.

'Hey,' announced Young Jim. 'That's the police car. Wonder why it's parked down here?'

'Maybe there's trouble up the gully,' said Elaine.

Young Jim shook his head. 'We'd have heard some commotion or other on the way down the track. You can't miss someone as big as Sergeant Ryan. No, look, here are his footprints in the sand, too. He's gone down the creek, not up towards the gully.'

'How do you know they're his footprints?' demanded Elaine. 'They could be the Williams boys', or Gully Jack's, or Dad's.'

''Cause no-one else round here wears boots, chookbrain. Not boots like his.'

'Maybe he's tracking bandits,' said Elaine eagerly. 'They've just stolen a thousand pounds and they're hiding in the valley.'

'Who'd they steal a thousand pounds from?' argued Young Jim. 'No-one here's got sixpence to spend on their tombstones. I bet there isn't even a thousand pennies in the whole valley.'

'Well, I don't know.'

'Maybe they stole it from Sydney and brought it down here,' suggested Barbara.

Elaine beamed at her. 'That's it. It was a daring bank robbery.'

'I think you've both got rats in your attic,' said Young Jim frankly. 'I bet he's just gone picking mushrooms or something.'

Elaine giggled. 'What would Sergeant Ryan want with mushrooms? He doesn't even cook.'

'Well I don't know,' said Young Jim, exasperated. 'How about we follow him upstream and see?'

Elaine shrugged. 'It's all right with me. I didn't want to go eeling anyway.'

'Bubba?'

'Sure.'

'Better take your shoes off,' advised Young Jim. 'You'll ruin them if you slip in the water. Here, give them to me. I'll stick them in my pocket.'

'It's okay. I can carry them.'

'You don't have a pocket. Here, hand them over,' ordered Young Jim. He bent down and looked at the boot prints again. 'Come on, everyone. Follow me.'

They walked slowly up the edge of the creek. The soil felt strange on Barbara's bare feet, worn hard and flat from floods, scattered with casuarina needles and sewn into a patchwork by eroded tree roots. The dragons stared at them, drowsy on their rocks, or leapt startled into the clear water and lay watchful on the bottom of the pools.

'We should check the opposite bank,' whispered Elaine. 'Maybe he followed the gangsters into the scrub.'

'Look, you silly fruit-bat,' said Young Jim. 'His footprints are just in front of us. Why are you whispering, anyway?'

'In case the gangsters hear us.'

'You and your bally gangsters. You've got gangsters on the brain. I bet Sergeant Ryan's never followed a gangster in his life. Chook thieves and drunk and disorderlies are more his line — look, there he is now.'

Sergeant Ryan was sitting on a rock that some forgotten flood had wedged in the exposed roots of a giant casuarina. He held a pencil that moved slowly and erratically over the book on his knee. He seemed oblivious to the approaching children.

'He can't hear us over the creek,' said Young Jim. 'Hey, Sergeant Ryan!'

Sergeant Ryan started. He closed the book quickly and put the pencil in his pocket. He stood.

'Afternoon,' he said awkwardly. 'You kiddies going for a walk?'

'We were going eeling,' said Elaine. 'But then we saw the car. We wondered what was up.'

Sergeant Ryan looked embarrassed.

'It's my afternoon off,' he told them, as though that explained what he was doing sitting up the creek.

Elaine looked at the book in his hand.

'What's that, Sergeant Ryan?'

Young Jim kicked her ankle.

'Don't be rude,' he hissed.

'Well, he doesn't have to tell me if he doesn't want to,' argued Elaine.

Sergeant Ryan looked even more embarrassed. He

fumbled with the book as though he wished he had a pocket big enough to hide it in.

'It's nothing,' he told them, trying to sound firm.

Elaine's eyes opened wide. 'I know what it is! It's a sketchbook. Mrs Henderson's got one from when she used to teach drawing at the school. I didn't know you sketched, Sergeant Ryan!' She plucked the book from Sergeant Ryan's grasp before he knew what had hit him.

'Hey, don't snatch,' objected Young Jim. 'Don't you have any respect for your elders? Ma'd have your hide if she saw what you just did.'

Elaine stuck her tongue out. 'Sez you. I just want to have a look. I *can* have a look, can't I, Sergeant Ryan?'

Sergeant Ryan looked at her helplessly. 'They're not much good,' he protested.

'I bet they are! Hey Bubba, have a look at this!'

Sergeant Ryan sighed.

Young Jim tried not to laugh. 'Ma says you need two brooms and a cage of tigers to keep Elaine from doing what she wants to,' he said.

'Too right,' said Sergeant Ryan. 'Look, kids, take a dekko if you really want,' he said. 'But you've got to promise me you won't go telling anyone, will you?'

'Why not?'

'Not even Dulcie?'

'Especially not Dulcie.' Sergeant Ryan shook his head. 'What do you think the blokes in the valley'd say if they knew their Sergeant drew pictures for a hobby? They'd laugh their heads off.'

Young Jim looked at him with sudden comprehension. 'You're right there,' he agreed.

Barbara looked over Elaine's shoulder at the sketchbook. The sketches were all in pencil. Most were views of the valley: the single tree on the hill above Dulcie's front paddock; a pool in the creek below the casuarinas. There was a sketch of the pub, and the post office and telephone exchange. There was a sketch of a strange house too, with a bull-nosed verandah, neat gardens and a picket fence. Barbara looked up. 'Where's this one?' she asked.

Young Jim peered over her shoulder. 'It looks like Dulcie's,' he said. 'But Dulcie's hasn't got a verandah — and the garden's not like this at all.' He looked up with sudden comprehension. 'It's like the one above Dulcie's mantelpiece!' he exclaimed. 'The one she thought Gully Jack did! But it was you, wasn't it?'

Sergeant Ryan looked embarrassed. 'It wasn't much,' he muttered.

'Hey, that's Dulcie with a baby — and this one's of you and Dulcie dancing.' Young Jim stared at Sergeant Ryan. 'But you've never been to any of the dances!'

Sergeant Ryan was silent.

'They're your dreams, aren't they?' said Young Jim quietly. Sergeant Ryan looked uncomfortable. 'Cripes, we've all got dreams. Dreams are things so close to you you think you'd die sometimes if anyone knew what they were.'

'What're your dreams then?' asked Elaine curiously.

'None of your beeswax,' said Young Jim shortly. He handed the book back to Sergeant Ryan. He hesitated. 'Sergeant Ryan, why don't you go to the dances? They're really beaut, and the food's just great, all sorts of cakes and pies and sandwiches and things. Dulcie would love it if you went.'

'I can't dance,' said Sergeant Ryan simply.

Young Jim stared at him. 'Everyone can dance,' he protested. 'Didn't your parents ever teach you?'

Sergeant Ryan shook his head. 'My Ma died,' he explained. 'And my Pa was more interested in the pub than teaching me to dance. There weren't any dances out our way anyway when I was young. Later,' he shrugged, 'I reckon I was too embarrassed to say I didn't know how.'

'Stone the blooming crows,' whistled Elaine. 'A sergeant who can't dance! Hey, it sounds like a song: The Dancing Sergeant.'

Sergeant Ryan's face went red.

'I can't dance either,' Barbara admitted softly.

Young Jim stared at her. 'You can't dance either! Cripes!' He grinned suddenly. 'Well, you know what then?'

'What?'

'We'll have to bally well show you, won't we then?'

'None of that language, boy,' said Sergeant Ryan. But his eyes were full of hope.

SERGEANT RYAN DANCES

It was like he'd fallen into the creek and come out in another world, where all the rules were different. It was like a dream had swept down with the breeze and carried him along. What was he doing here by the creek, wondered Sergeant Ryan — on a grassy flat, kept short by roos and wallabies, watched by kookaburras and blooming water dragons, dancing with a mob of kids?

'Come on, lift your boots,' ordered Elaine. 'One, two, three, one, two, three — hey, he's nearly got it, hasn't he?'

Young Jim twirled Barbara around a log of driftwood topped with wombat droppings. 'You're doing great! Let's try the polka again. You remember how it goes Bubba — to the right, no follow me, you great galah — and lift your feet, dad dah dah dah dah, careful, don't trip over that rock, dah dah dah da dah, dah dah — dahdah, dumde dumde, that's the way!'

'My feet keep getting tangled!'

'Then lift them up, you nitwit. That's the way.'

'Watch out for the tree root, Sergeant Ryan, now back again and turn around.'

'Ow!'

'I said watch out for the tree root. It's all right, Sergeant Ryan, there won't be any tree roots in the hall tonight. Come on, try it again.'

The sun was leaning on the casuarinas when they'd finished, puffing and giggling.

'Think you can manage now?' demanded Elaine, standing back with her hands on her hips.

'I think I can manage anything after that,' said Sergeant Ryan.

'You'd better,' Elaine warned him. 'Or I'll have to come down to the police station and show you again.'

'Cripes,' said Young Jim suddenly. 'We forgot all about lunch. Where's the swag, I'm starved! And Ma is expecting those eels for tea.'

'I'll give you a hand,' said Sergeant Ryan. 'I may not be much of a dancer, but I do know about eels. And there's a big slab of fruit cake back in the car. Old Ma Hourigan at the pub makes a good fruit cake.'

'You're a real beaut dancer,' said Elaine. She grinned. 'I'm a bonzer teacher.'

They rock-hopped back down the edge of the creek to the eel pond. Sergeant Ryan glanced at Young Jim, intent on placing his feet on the slippery rocks.

'You know — what you were saying about dreams and all that — well, if there's anything I can ever do to give you a hand. I mean, I know it's hard for a kid like you.'

Young Jim looked at him for a moment. His eyes were a brighter blue, as though he was considering. Then he shook his head. 'No,' he said. 'I reckon my dream's — well, just a dream. But thank you anyway.' They walked in silence for a minute. 'You'll be coming to the dance then, tonight?'

Sergeant Ryan grinned, 'What'd you say if I said no?'

'I'd say we'd come down the valley and drag you up here,' said Elaine frankly. 'I didn't get trodden on by your great boots for nothing.'

'I reckon that'd be against the law,' said Young Jim. 'That'd be assaulting an officer, wouldn't it Sergeant Ryan?'

Sergeant Ryan nodded. 'Too right,' he agreed. 'I'd hate to see you land in gaol, missy. I reckon I'll just have to turn up to keep you safe.'

Dinner was early that night, the sun still hovering above the ridge and the shadows spreading long and thick from the trees. It was roast mutton, the forequarter Gully Jack had given them the day before, baked in their home-made oven set at the edge of the clearing — a kero tin packed in a bed of clay and ants' nest, with a rough firebox on either side. The firebox was two big holes dug into the clay with holes at the top for the smoke.

Ma had decided to keep the eels for the next night. They sat in a kero tin of salty water around the back of the shanty, gutted and twisted, 'Looking just like meat,' as Barbara said wonderingly, not like the savage snake-like things they'd fished out of the creek.

The girls had stayed by the fire ever since they'd got home, feeding it with more twigs and bits of bark to keep it hot and the dinner cooking evenly. The meat smelt wonderful. There was even gravy, made in the camp oven from the dripping and browned flour and water, and potatoes in their jackets cooked in the ashes, and boiled pumpkin and swedes and beans, as much as anyone could eat.

'No point leaving it for the bandicoots,' said Dad, passing his plate over for a second helping. 'You know love, I reckon you're the best cook in New South Wales. I bet you could cook a drover's dog and make it taste like chicken.'

'That's what Gully Jack says,' said Elaine. 'He says he wished he had someone like Ma to cook for him.'

'Then he'd better marry Dulcie before they both turn grey,' said Ma. 'Thellie and Joey, if you don't eat your pumpkin there won't be any pudding. It's treacle dumplings, but there won't be a single crumb for anyone who doesn't eat their vegies.'

The sun collapsed behind the ridges like someone had burst it and let all the air out. The shadows spread across the hills. Young Jim covered the fire with old ashes to keep the coals burning for the morning and to stop sparks spreading, and plucked his good shirt from the thornbush. It was dry now and smelt faintly of creek and gum leaves. Ma checked that everyone had brushed their teeth, with twigs dipped into a cup of salt and rubbed in firmly until their gums were red and their teeth as shiny as bits of quartz in the sunlight.

'Hey Ma, could you cut my hair?'

'Not now.' Ma's head was in the box where she kept her good clothes, wrapped in brown paper and mothballs. 'There isn't time.'

'But Ma, it's shaggy as a balding budgie.'

'You should have thought of it earlier.'

Dad was shaving with the last of the hot water left over from tea, squinting into the tiny mirror balanced on a tree branch. He scraped off a week's worth of whiskers.

'Struth, I wish I'd done this earlier, the light'll be gone in a minute.'

'Ma, Joey took my underpants.'

'No they're not, they're mine!'

'Says who?'

'If you two don't shut up I'll spiflicate the both of you.' Elaine was trying to plait her hair. 'Has anyone seen my good ribbon?'

'You just watch your language my girl.'

'It's there in front of you, dopey!'

'No it's not.'

'It's right there. Struth, if it was a dog it'd bite you!'

'Can someone spread tomato jam on those pikelets I made for supper?'

'Oh Ma, not tomato jam, no-one'll eat it. How about the apple jelly?'

'Ma, I have to go to the toilet!'

'Well, off you go then.'

'It's getting dark. I'm scared.'

'I'll take you then.' Barbara took Thellie's sticky hand. 'You've been licking the treacle tin, haven't you?'

'How do you know?' Thellie licked the brown stains from around her lips. 'I bet you know everything Bubba, don't you? I'm glad you're my sister now.'

Barbara smiled. 'Why?'

''Cause you tell good stories. Tell me about the funny boxes, again Bubba. The ones that tell you stories too.'

Thellie skipped along the narrow path. The dunny was in the bush behind the shack, modestly hidden behind the thornbushes — three poles upright in the ground and another two strapped on to them longways, with bark woven in between for walls and a deep pit in the middle that had taken two days to dig. The seat was a kero tin with a hole in it and a big sheet of bark was filled with dry moss, used instead of toilet paper. There was no roof. 'I mean what's the use,' Elaine had said when she showed it to Barbara. 'If it's raining you get as wet walking down there as you do sitting on the seat and thinking.'

Barbara waited outside until Thellie had finished and washed her hands in the tin of water that Ma kept filled beside the bark. The air smelt faintly of dunny and gum leaves and sweet night air, a different smell from daytime, different from any smell she'd known before. A wallaby crashed by, then stopped and peered into the growing dusk, as though wondering if there was someone there or not. Its whiskers twitched and it hopped on.

'Bubba, I'm finished now.' Thellie took Barbara's hand again. 'Do you think anyone will dance with you?' she asked.

'I don't know,' said Barbara honestly. 'Are you going to dance?'

'People always ask me to dance,' said Thellie importantly, 'Dad, and Joey 'cause Dad tells him that he's got to, and Gully Jack danced with me last time, when Mrs Reynolds took a turn on the piano. I was the only one he asked to dance in the whole room except for Dulcie. You get to dance with everyone in the barn dance.'

The chaos in the clearing had subsided when they got back. Ma was flushed, in her best dress kept pressed in brown paper for Friday nights; Dad was pink-faced and dewhiskered. Elaine was resplendent in the ribbons she only wore once a week. It was hard to recognise her with her hair tidy and not waving around her face like a swarm of butterflies. Young Jim was in his clean shirt and his sandshoes, not bare feet, and the little ones had clean bright faces. Dad counted heads. 'All ready then? We're off.'

There wasn't room on the track for everyone at once. The little ones skipped in front with Dad and Ma arm in arm behind, Young Jim carrying Harry piggyback on his shoulders, and Elaine carrying the pikelets Ma had made, spread with apple jelly from Dulcie's apples, to add to supper. The lamps were lit in the other shanties. Shadows hunted for clean clothes or their last pair of boots, put away for occasions such as this. Down the track they could hear the voices of other parties wending their way towards the hall.

'What's up?' Young Jim spoke softly to Barbara.

'Nothing. Just a bit scared.'

'What of? It's a dance! You're supposed to enjoy yourself.'

'I don't know. Just the idea of so many strangers, I suppose.'

'Don't worry. You just stick with me and you'll be right. Hey, there's Mr Henderson. Mr Henderson, aren't you coming?'

'Maybe he can't dance either?' whispered Barbara.

Young Jim stared. 'Of course he can dance. He's a school teacher isn't he?'

The Hendersons were sitting by their camp fire watching the flames. Mr Henderson squinted through the darkness. He hesitated before he spoke. 'It's Young Jim O'Reilly isn't it? No, not tonight, son. I can't say we're in the mood for dancing.'

'But you've got to come.' Elaine was bouncing with excitement. '*Everyone* is coming. Come on, you'll love it when you're there.'

Mr Henderson glanced at his wife.

'I don't have a good dress to wear any more,' she said uncertainly. 'I thought I had them all packed safely but when I went to look they'd all got mildewed ...' Her voice broke off.

'What's a bit of mildew?' Ma's voice was matter-of-fact. 'You bring it up tomorrow and we'll have a go with salt and lemon juice. There's a lemon tree laden with fruit down by Dulcie's. The kids can pick a few of them. Anyway, you look lovely as you are, doesn't she Dad?'

'Pretty as a sackful of sugar to a hive full of bees,' agreed Dad.

It was as though something in the air had infected Mr Henderson. He smiled uncertainly at his wife. 'In that case, why not!'

'That's the spirit that won the Empire,' said Dad. Mr Henderson was still smiling as he kicked ash over the fire and held out his hand to his wife.

The hall was lit by kero lanterns, shadows jumping crazily as figures strolled out of the darkness, past bright yellow windows and walls too dark to see the peeling paint on them. Posters were plastered by the door:

All Talkie Features, first Monday of each month; Herbert Rowe Presents his

Original Refined and Entertaining Musical Comedy Show, prices 2/-, 3/-.

Children half price.

Kids played hopscotch out the side by the dim squares of light from the windows. Men were clustered by the steps yarning about the weather or the death of Phar Lap, women perched chatting on the verandah rails, and horses whickered from the yard behind. Through at the back of the hall, Barbara could see Dulcie with the other valley women, setting plates along the trestles that had been covered by a selection of multicoloured cloths. Flowers tumbled out of vases under the faded streamers and the tinted photo of the King.

'Where's the music?' she whispered.

Young Jim looked around. 'Gully Jack'll be along soon. He'll have kept digging till dark. You can't get Gully Jack away from his diggings while there's any light. He likes to wait till the hall's filled up before he starts to play anyway.'

'He plays the piano?'

'Naw. Remember? He'd have your guts for garters if he heard you say that. He's got his fiddle. Loud enough to wake the kookaburras, you wait and see. As long as he gets his whisky he'll play all night.'

'Who brings the whisky?'

'Johnny Halloran goes up to town each week with the vegie cart. Everyone throws in something, a few tomatoes or some rabbits. He sells them and gets the whisky for tonight. Come on.'

Barbara held back, her eyes wide at all the people. Who would have thought there were so many tucked among the wattles and gums and thornbush.

'What's up?'

'I'm nervous, that's all. What if I can't remember the steps?'

'You'll remember. Who cares about the steps anyway? Think about the food.'

The inside of the hall was lit by the glow of lanterns and it was hot, a reminder of the day's sun that had baked the walls and roof. Gully Jack was in his corner in a shirt with all its buttons. His face was shiny, scraped clean of black whiskers, his eyes blue as the morning sky. A chipped teacup by his side had been filled with a pale brown liquid. The fiddle lay across his knees as he tested the strings, ting tung, tung.

'Take your partners!'

'Come on, Bubba, they'll be starting without us!' Young Jim pulled Barbara on to the floor before she could object. Ma was there already with Dad, and Thellie with Joey, his face looking sulky, as though Dad had already had a word with him and told him to dance with his sister, and Elaine stood with a boy from down the valley, his big bare feet still grubby from the dusty track and knees like a kangaroo's. Even Mr Henderson was there, looking surprised at enjoying himself, with his arm around his wife's waist, her hair gleaming in the lamplight, her happy face looking years younger than it had half an hour before.

There was a surprised stirring at the door. 'Hey, there's Sergeant Ryan,' whispered Barbara.

The dancers fell silent as Sergeant Ryan walked slowly into the hall, as though they wondered why he had come, for pleasure or on official business. Sergeant Ryan looked self-conscious and uncomfortable. It was the first time Barbara had seen him out of his uniform. His hair was slicked back so tight it seemed to be made of leather and his face shone bright. He looked nervously around the room.

'I knew he'd come,' said Young Jim, satisfied. 'He'd never hear the last of it from Elaine if he hadn't.'

Sergeant Ryan caught Dulcie's eye among the teacups. He threw his shoulders back and marched across the hall as if he was on parade, as though unaware that every eye was on him.

Dulcie put down the teapot she'd been filling. She smiled slowly, like someone finding a Christmas present where they had least expected it, hidden behind the tree. She put her hand out to Sergeant Ryan, and he reached over the trestles and took it.

Barbara glanced at Gully Jack. He was frowning. He held his fiddle against his waist, as though wondering whether to put it down.

'Hey, where's the flaming music?' The yell came from somewhere at the front of the hall.

Gully Jack lifted his fiddle to his chin as Sergeant Ryan led Dulcie into the centre of the hall. She placed her hand on his shoulder. Gully Jack took a deep gulp from his teacup before he lifted up his bow.

'Bluurrk! What the ...' Gully Jack spat the brown liquid frantically all over the floor, and glared around the room. 'This is flamin' tea! Where's me flamin' whisky?'

'Shhh,' said someone, glancing towards Sergeant Ryan, who looked carefully out the door as though he couldn't hear.

'Where's me whisky?' demanded Gully Jack again, glaring at Dulcie and Sergeant Ryan and the hall in general. 'It's Friday flamin' night and I don't play without me flamin' whisky.'

'There isn't any flamin' whisky!'

'Why not?'

'Because Johnny Halloran broke his leg when the cart

turned over coming back from town and Doc gave it to him to stop the pain while he set it, that's why.'

The hall was silent. Gully Jack gazed around the room at the crowd of dancers. At the men in creek-washed shirts, at the women in their Friday night dresses, at the wide-eyed kids in bare feet or tattered sandshoes.

Gully Jack took another gulp from the teacup. 'S'pose a bloke could get used to tea on Friday nights,' he said, and lifted up his bow.

The music filled the night.

It was a night like none that Barbara had experienced before. The hall shook as feet pounded to the music. It was as if the world was fast, but slow, at the same time. Up the hall and down again, and galloping all around, swung from partner to partner in the barn dance until she lost count, tripping over Sergeant Ryan's boots till he laughed at her and swirled her off her feet.

Susso or cocky, it didn't matter, not tonight. Men with untrimmed whiskers tangling in their shirt buttons and sweat running down their faces, with laughing women who had forgotten the tin shantytown across the creek, the damper they would make for breakfast, the bread they had to measure so it would last, and kids with more bounce than skill. The music talked to them all, always the music. The magic thread of Gully Jack's fiddle timed the beat of feet and clap of hands. It soared over the children's giggles, and the shrieks of the possums up in the ceiling, their quiet evening gone.

'See, I said it'd be fun,' Young Jim panted. 'And there's still the best bit to come. You wait till you taste supper. Dulcie organises that.'

Barbara looked down to the hearth at the back of the hall. Dulcie was there again, checking a big kero tin of boiling water. She lifted it off the heat and threw some tea leaves in and began to ladle out cup after cup — chipped cups of a dozen colours, collected from every household in the valley that had any to spare.

'Hey, come on!' Young Jim grabbed Barbara's hand. 'The best tucker'll be gone before we get there!'

Supper was cold mutton and chutney on thick white bread, plus pikelets, pumpkin fritters, fairy cakes with soft fresh cream, apple teacake fragrant with nutmeg, sponge cake with plum jam and cream, and trifle with jam and fresh sliced peaches and more cream. Dulcie gathered a cup of tea and plate of cake. She said something softly to Sergeant Ryan, then headed down to where Gully Jack still sat with his fiddle. He nodded to her, wiping the sweat from his neck and took the hot fresh tea. He seemed about to speak.

'Hey Jack, how's that channel doing, you getting near the seam yet?' Old Man Lee's hands were wrapped around a buttered scone.

Gully Jack's eyes lit up. 'Getting closer.' He put down his cup of tea. 'I reckon I've got it this time. Another month or two and she'll be there. You know what I think? I reckon ...'

Dulcie stood ignored with the plate of cake in her hand. Her face was half-sad, half-tolerant. She put the plate down by Gully Jack's elbow and walked back down the hall towards Sergeant Ryan.

Sergeant Ryan was waiting for her. He handed her a fresh cup of tea with a fairy cake on the saucer, and led her out to the cool air of the verandah till the music began again.

'May I have the pleasure?' Barbara looked up. It was Mr Henderson, smiling down at her, his big teeth yellow in the lamplight. Barbara shook her head nervously. 'It's a waltz, isn't it? I don't think I know how to waltz well enough.'

It was different dancing with Young Jim — he didn't care how many mistakes she made. She looked around. Young Jim was still outside, telling a mob of boys from down the valley about the demonstration and the Unemployed Workers Union, the opening of the Harbour Bridge and how he'd seen Jack Lang once up in Sydney.

Mr Henderson grinned. He had a nice grin. His big teeth stuck out again, long and shiny in the lamplight. 'Every girl needs to learn to waltz. Just follow my feet. One two three and one two three and one two three.'

Suddenly it was easy. Around and around the room they flashed. The possums shrieked up in the roof as the floor shook with the dancing, one two three, one two three. Gully Jack's eyes gleamed brighter than the lanterns as his elbow flashed and he dreamed of his gullies. One two three, one two three.

The moon was sinking behind the ridges as they walked back home, up the narrow path between the thornbushes. Over on the track she could hear the sound of cartwheels, the clop of horses and the burp of someone's car. Ma was walking arm-in-arm with Dad and she was singing, too softly to hear the words, gentle as the mumble of the creek. The little ones straggled behind, holding on to skirts and arms so as not to lose each other in the shadows.

'Tired?'

Barbara smiled at Young Jim. He was carrying Harry piggyback again. Harry drooped, dozing on his shoulder. 'No. My head's still dancing. One two three, one two three.'

'Yeah, I saw you dancing with old Henderson. Who'd have thought he could dance like that? But it was fun, wasn't it?'

Barbara nodded. 'The best fun I think I've had in my entire life.'

Young Jim grinned. She could just see the flash of his teeth in the moonlight. 'Till next week anyway. There's another dance then, don't forget.' He yawned deeply, stretching so hard his shirt ripped at the back. 'Crikey! Well, it lasted for the dance anyway. Maybe Ma can patch it up tomorrow. Come on, let's get home. I'm really whacked.'

An owl began to call, very far away, then the noise faded in the bubble of the creek. Like her old life, thought Barbara sleepily, fading all the time, until all that was left were the O'Reillys and the smell of night and leaves and strands of bark and the shack that was home.

SATURDAY

Everyone slept late the Saturday after the dance. The tin roof cracked as the hot sun struck it, the cicadas yelled in the trees and the flies buzzed around the ashes of the fire as though they could still smell the food that had been cooked on it.

Dad rose first, stretching, and kindled the fire with bits of twig and bark until the billy's steam mingled with the smoke. The little ones tumbled out still bleary-eyed and yawning, with Elaine and Young Jim and Barbara slowly coming after them.

Dad handed Elaine a cup of tea. 'You take that into your Ma. She's properly worn out.'

'Too much dancing,' yawned Elaine.

'Too much looking after you lot,' said Dad. 'Don't you be nagging at her to get up and make breakfast either.'

'You making breakfast then, Dad?' asked Elaine unbelievingly. 'What're you going to make, snake legs on biscuits?'

'None of your lip, my girl. It'll be fried bread in last night's dripping, and there's tomato jam in the box. The King of England would be glad of a breakfast like that, may his socks rot on his feet. But what would he need a good breakfast for with a soft life like his?'

The bread browned and crisped in the old black pan and the dripping spat and spluttered in the heat, bringing back the memories of last night's roast, as it melted into the scents of warm rock and gum trees.

Barbara spread the tomato jam thickly for the little ones, and bit into her bread. It was hot and hard and tasted meaty. Slowly the fire died down to a bed of coals that winked red and black in their grey surrounds. The billy rested at the edges.

'How did you enjoy the dance, Bubba?' asked Dad, toasting another bit of bread on a long green stick. 'Young Jim here look after you all right?'

'It was the first dance I've ever been to,' said Barbara. 'At least the first dance like that. Is there really a dance every week?'

'Too right,' said Dad. 'You've got to have some fun in life, even in a place like this. Not that this is such a bad place. If things were different you could make a good life here. Ah well, if I put my dreams in one hand and spat in the other I know which one'd be full first.'

Elaine giggled. 'You could try walking round Barbara's corner,' she suggested. 'You know what I'd have if I could walk round the corner?'

'What?' asked Young Jim seriously from over by the fire.

'I'd have a great big room with a thousand books in it, all mine and no-one else's, with clean white pages that no-one else's fingers had ever touched. I'd have carpet so thick on the floor you could roll in it.'

Thellie giggled.

'And no brats to wash, either,' added Elaine, giving Thellie's hair a tweak. 'You come here, brat, and I'll clean your face for you. You could grow potatoes in it. What would you have, Jim?'

Young Jim ran his hands through his pale hair. 'Dunno,' he said shortly. 'What's the use of dreaming?'

'Oh, go on,' said Elaine. 'Just imagine we could walk round the corner. Where would you go?'

Young Jim glanced at her. He seemed to come to a decision. 'I'd be changing the world,' he said slowly. 'That's what I'd be doing. I'd be out there fighting with Jack Lang and all the rest of them. I'd be finding out why some people have so much and others don't have blankets on their beds. But I'd need an education for that. I'd need to know about things.'

'Garn. All you need's your soapbox,' said Elaine. 'Then you could climb up on it and yack away all you want to.'

Young Jim opened his mouth to argue.

'I'd have a hairyplane,' Thellie interrupted, bouncing up and down.

'You mean an aeroplane, you silly bandicoot,' said Elaine.

'That's what I said, a big one just like Bubba had, and I'd have lots of ice-creams.'

'I'd have four thousand sausages,' said Joey.

'You'd be sick!'

'No, I wouldn't. I'd have chops for breakfast every morning, too.'

The hessian doorflap opened and Ma came out slowly, tying back her hair and straightening her dress.

'What would you have, Ma?' demanded Elaine.

'What do you mean?' Ma's voice was still sleepy.

'We're pretending we could all go round corners like Bubba did. I want a whole room of books and Jim wants to change the world — or at least make speeches to everyone in it — and Thellie wants aeroplanes.'

'I'd have a house.' Ma spoke dreamily, as though she didn't know what she was saying. 'A house with a real roof on it and a kitchen with a stove, and a school for all of you ... a good school so you could get a decent education ...' She saw Dad's face and broke off. 'And if wishes were fishes we'd all be rich. All I really want's a cuppa. Is there water in the billy, love? That bread smells good.'

Dad poured her a cup of tea without speaking. Elaine glanced at his hard-set face, at Ma's careful lack of expression.

'Come on,' she said to Barbara. 'Let's take the dishes and the littl'uns down to the creek, and get the lot of them clean. You coming, Jim?'

Young Jim nodded without speaking. They walked down the track in silence.

DAD AND MR HENDERSON

Dad watched them as they disappeared down the track. His kids — his wonderful strong kids — stuck here in the bush without a chance, without a future, and there was nothing he could do about it.

Maybe it was the letdown from the dance, maybe it was Bubba's stories, making you think the world might be different one day, just around the corner. Dad didn't know. All he knew was he couldn't settle, couldn't sit still, couldn't stand to see Ma's face, so resolutely cheerful. He was too restless even to go and water the tomatoes, though they needed it. The poor things would be wilting in this sun, the lettuces too.

Ma looked up. She was crocheting one of her rugs again, bright strips of rag that would be a hearthrug, or a kitchen mat when Johnny Halloran sold it in town. But Johnny Halloran had broken his leg, Dad remembered. There'd be no more trips to town for weeks maybe.

'Settle down,' suggested Ma, trying to sound normal. 'Why don't you put the billy on. We'll have a cuppa on our ownsome before the mob comes back to annoy us.'

Dad shook his head, but he stirred up the fire anyway.

He scooped a billy of water out of the kero tin in the shade. The billy sizzled in the hot ashes. Elaine's voice rose from down by the creek, calling the little ones to order. A child laughed, and called something back.

'Listen to them.' Dad's voice was harsh.

Ma looked up from her stitching. 'They're healthy. They're happy. They've got a roof over their heads and full bellies. There are others a lot worse off.'

'They should be at school. They should be making something of themselves.'

'Things'll get better.' Ma's voice was as comforting as she could make it, with just a hint of fear below.

'Yeah, the good times are just around the corner.' Dad smiled grimly. 'That's what the newspapers say, isn't it.' That's what Bubba said happened to her. She'd just stepped somewhere around the corner. He knew what would be around the corner if he had his way — a better world — one that had a future for his kids. A school, teachers; he could see it so clearly he could almost taste it.

Teachers ...

The shadows seemed to shiver slightly. Dad looked up, startled. The sun must have come out from behind a cloud, but there weren't any clouds today.

Ma was looking at him strangely. 'What is it?'

Dad brought his fist down so hard the table rattled on its stones. 'Struth, I've been flaming blind! Blind as a bat in the midday flaming sun! We've got a flaming teacher!'

'What do you mean?'

'Old Henderson! He's a teacher isn't he? I bet his wife could teach as well.'

'But—'

'But nothing.' Dad surged to his feet.

'Where are you going?' Ma started to run after him.

'I'm going to start a flaming school. That's where I'm going.' He laughed suddenly. 'If I'm late for lunch you lot start without me. Tell the kids I've gone for a little walk — just a stroll around the flaming corner!'

MR HENDERSON

It was too hot to stay in the tent, with the flies buzzing like tiny engines. He got up and dressed as quietly as he could, so as not to wake Marge, still sleeping on the pile of blankets. She looked so peaceful, the lines of strain softened from her face. How long had it been since she'd enjoyed herself like she had last night? It must be a year or more since they'd danced together.

Mr Henderson put his hand over the ashes. They were stone cold. He'd have to start the fire again before they could have breakfast, but what did it matter, there was all the time in the world. Nothing to do but get more wood, or haul the water, or pan for gold and hope somehow for a miracle, a gleam of colour in his pan.

He reached over to the woodpile. That's one thing about this place, there was plenty of wood if you were cold, and plenty of rabbits if you were hungry, if you liked eating rabbit. He never had. But you got used to it, just like you got used to living in a tent, and the loss of all the life you'd known.

The wood was damp from the dew, but there was dry wood further down the pile. Mr Henderson pushed it with his foot before he took a piece, careful of snakes and spiders. Red-bellied blacks loved woodpiles. He remembered the first one they'd seen, about fifteen years ago now. They'd been married a year and he'd been a headmaster for two. It was their first holiday together, unless you counted their honeymoon in the mountains.

Camping had been fun then, the washing in cold water in the creek, Marge giggling when a bowerbird stole the soap, cooking on an open fire, the bright flames licking at the air. It was all fun, even when the black snake crawled out from behind the log they'd been sitting on and Marge had screamed, then laughed, because the snake was obviously much more scared of them. Camping was fun when you knew you had a house to go back to, a proper stove, a bathroom, good gas lights, a job where people looked up to you, security and money in the bank.

The job went first, and then the house. The house went with the job. Then their savings, gradually eaten away, until they knew that if they kept paying rent the money would be gone and they'd have nothing. Then the bank had shut. So they had come here. He'd thought he could make a bit fossicking, but the gold wasn't there. He supposed they were better off than most. At least they had the tent and the right equipment ... if only they had hope as well.

Hope seemed very far away, so far it seemed he'd never find it again.

A child yelled in the distance. One of the O'Reilly kids, or that new girl, Bubba, the one that thought she came from far away. From somewhere around the corner.

What *would* it be like to have another world around the corner, one that you could just step into if things got bad? Mr Henderson smiled to himself. He thought about walking around the corner of the track down to town, and there would be a school where Dulcie's washhouse was now. There'd be desks inside and ink wells, and the ink monitor busy filling them up before the lessons started.

There'd be slates for the young ones that squeaked when they wrote on them, and the grey dust would stain their fingers as they learnt their letters and their sums. There'd be a blackboard and a desk out front, and he'd keep his favourite books inside and read to them on sleepy afternoons or when it was too wet to go outside; all the books he'd loved when he was young that he could share with them.

That was the joy of teaching, knowing you opened up new worlds for the kids. All they had to do was reach out and grab it, just take those first few steps around the corner.

He could almost see it, that school. The kids would be lined up at the door, elbowing each other to get in first, as though it really mattered. He could almost hear their footsteps as they marched inside, tramp tramp tramp.

Mr Henderson opened his eyes. They weren't children's steps, they were the steps of an adult. He saw O'Reilly from up the creek heading through the clearing. Mr Henderson looked up and tried to pretend he hadn't been dreaming.

'Morning.'

Dad nodded. He stood uncertainly, wondering where to start, rubbing his great hands together.

'Sit down.'

Dad pulled up an old kero tin, padded with sacking and sat.

'You'll think I'm crazy,' he began slowly, 'but I got this

idea. It seemed to come from nowhere, but once it took hold—'

'What idea?' asked Mr Henderson.

'About a school.'

'There isn't any school in Poverty Gully.' Mr Henderson's voice was hard.

'I know there's not a school. It breaks my heart to see the kids sometimes, no learning, no future. All they know is what they can see here. It's just not good enough.'

Mr Henderson didn't meet his eyes. 'They can go up to town. There's a school there. A good school.'

'Two hours away if you've got a horse, or the money to board your kids, and no-one here's got money like that.' Dad broke off. 'I reckon I'm not telling you anything you don't know.'

'No,' said Mr Henderson shortly. Out of the corner of his eye he could see Marge slip through the tent flaps. She just stood there, not joining in.

'So I was thinking, why can't we start a school?' Dad held up his hand. 'No, don't say anything yet. I know we don't have a proper building. But I went down to Dulcie's — you know, Dulcie at the dairy farm. Well, she's got an old washhouse. It's not much but it's got a proper floor and everything, and it's got a kitchen at the back of it. It used to be the old kitchen before they built the main house. It's even got the old stove in it.

'Well, I know it's not much now, but we could mend the roof and clean it up a bit.'

Mr Henderson was looking at him strangely. Dad rushed on. 'Well, I reckon we could make a pretty good school there if we tried.'

Mr Henderson's face was expressionless. Dad spoke more quietly now, trying to convince. 'I know we can't pay you proper wages — struth, most of us can't pay you anything at all — but we'll give what we can. We'll all chip in with vegies, rabbits, or whatever. You spend your time with our kids and we'll do what we can for you.'

Dad stopped in the face of Mr Henderson's silence. He stood up. 'I should have known it was too much to ask,' he said gruffly. 'A bloke like you would want a proper school. That's what you're waiting for, I know.'

'No, wait.' Mr Henderson grabbed his arm. 'You just took me by surprise, that's all. Marge, stick the billy on will you?'

Dad looked at him, hope in his eyes. 'I know it wouldn't be a proper school—'

'Why not?' Mr Henderson ran his hands through his hair. 'Why not make it a proper school? What else do we need? We've got the kids, we've got the building and I'm a damn good teacher, if I do say so myself. We'll make it a proper school.'

'But—'

'We'll write to the Department of Education. There's a scheme — I can't remember what it's called. If the parents provide board and lodging and a building, the government will give you a subsidy. It's not much, but it'd probably pay for books, and slates.' Mr Henderson slammed his fist into his hand. 'Even if they won't it doesn't matter. We'll write on flipping paperbark if we have to.' He turned to Marge. 'What do you think?'

There were tears in Marge's eyes, happy tears. 'I think we should go and see that washhouse.'

'Not a washhouse,' said Mr Henderson. 'From now on it's the Poverty Gully School. No, not Poverty Gully — just the Gully School. There'll be nothing poor about the education the kids get at this school.'

'We'll hold a meeting,' said Dad. 'We'll call everyone in the valley together. We'll get this thing organised. We'll ...'

Mr Henderson suddenly seemed to come down to earth. 'What if the valley people don't want a school? I haven't taught for over two years now. What if they don't want someone from a susso camp teaching their kids?'

Marge touched his shoulder. 'You hold your meeting,' she told him. 'We'll convince them somehow.' She laughed, high and happy, a younger, more excited sound than he'd heard from her in years. 'Then someone's going to have to break the news to the kids.'

MEETING

It was strange to see the hall filled with chairs, thought Barbara, not bare like it was for dancing. It looked different tonight. It felt different too: of expectation as thick as treacle, not the laughter of Friday night as the valley let its strain and worry fly out the door with the music of Gully Jack's fiddle.

Dance or meeting, though, the trestles at the back were still set up for supper, as though nothing could take place in the hall without cups of tea and plates of scones with apple jelly, and pikelets with quince jam.

Dad wore his best trousers, hauled out of the tea chest and draped over a bush until the smell of mothballs faded. Dad and Mr Henderson had argued over who was going to address the meeting first. They'd decided on Dad to begin with and Mr Henderson second. Ma and Marge Henderson had taken their husband's trousers down to Dulcie's to use the iron. Mr Henderson even wore a coat and tie, the coat slightly shiny, but still good. You could smell the mothballs right down in the front seats.

'He looks like a teacher. Doesn't he?' Young Jim whispered to Barbara. She nodded. 'He wouldn't be bad, though,' she said, remembering the way he'd shown her how to waltz. 'I mean, he seems to like kids.'

'We must be mad,' said Elaine gloomily. 'I mean, who wants to go to blooming school anyway?' She shifted Thellie on her lap. 'Now you sit still, hear me or I'll have to take you outside and I'll miss Dad's speech.'

'You know, it's funny,' Young Jim spoke seriously. 'It's not like I *want* to go to school. It's just that I don't like not being able to go.'

Elaine tidied Thellie's hair. 'It's almost like I'm scared of school,' she said quietly. 'I mean I'd sort of accepted it, that I couldn't get my Leaving or even my Intermediate, that I'd just be like Ma, getting married and having kids. But now there's a chance of school again — and you find all your dreams come flooding in, as though I can choose what I want — and it's sort of frightening.'

Thellie wriggled again. 'Can't you sit still?' demanded Elaine. 'It's like having a bag of lizards on my lap.'

'Here, pass her over,' said Barbara. 'I'll hold her for a bit.'

Thellie held her arms out immediately.

'Tell me a story,' she ordered.

'I can't. Dad's going to talk in a minute. Look at all the people coming in instead.'

'I wonder what they're thinking,' whispered Elaine. 'It'll break Dad's heart if they don't want the school.'

'I think it'll hurt Mr Henderson worse,' said Young Jim sombrely. 'I mean, it'd be like they don't think he's a real teacher, just because he's a susso and lives in Poverty Gully.'

'But he is a real teacher,' objected Elaine. 'He's been a headmaster and everything.'

Young Jim looked at her.

'You haven't been up in Sydney lately,' he said. 'You should hear people talk about the sussos there. Like you don't exist once you're in a susso camp. People just want to shut their eyes, pretend it's your fault if you've lost your job. I tell you, it's real crook.'

Elaine sighed. 'Shut him up, someone. He'd talk the leg off an iron pot if you gave him half a chance.'

'A bloke can express an opinion, can't he?' demanded Young Jim.

'Go tell the gum trees,' advised Elaine. 'Look, there's still people coming. I didn't know there were so many families in the valley.'

The hall was slowly filling up with families from all along the valley who'd seen the notices down at the pub, or in the store, or up on Sergeant Ryan's notice board.

They were strangers' faces; men with thin legs and large hands, and eyes that were used to measuring from one end of a paddock to another; women with lipstick on, in their Sunday best. The footpath in front of the hall was filled with carts and battered vehicles and the whinnies of tethered horses. These people were the small farmers of the valley, burdened with low prices, the weight of last year's drought and the worry of the next; the farm workers; the eucy cutters, still carrying the sharp hot scent of eucalyptus oil from their stills; rabbit trappers; old Nicholson from the store, hard to recognise without his long white apron; and blonde Anna from the pub — they said she could tell if a man was going to swear ten seconds before he did and would quell him with one look.

Sergeant Ryan sat up the front with Dulcie, who had one eye on the water as it simmered above its kero burner.

'Where's Gully Jack?' whispered Barbara.

'Huh. Catch him spending a good Saturday afternoon indoors. Anyway, why should he care about the school?'

'I don't know.' Barbara felt suddenly forlorn. 'I thought he might care because of us.'

'Shush, Dad's going to speak.'

Dad stood on the raised platform at the front, under the photo of the King. He hitched his pants up nervously. He caught Ma's eye and seemed to gain confidence enough to speak.

'Uh, well, good afternoon ladies and gentlemen,' Dad began. 'I reckon you all know we're here because we don't have a school in the valley, and some of us think it's about time there was one.'

'There's never been a school in the valley.' It was old Nicholson's voice from the middle of the hall. 'Don't see why there has to be one now.'

There were murmurs of agreement around him. Mr Nicholson folded his arms belligerently and stared at Dad, as though affronted that a bloke from Poverty Gully would dare to use the stage.

Dad hitched his trousers up again. 'He needs to take his belt in another notch,' whispered Young Jim. 'Or maybe get some braces. He's got thinner since he last wore those.'

'I don't reckon it matters if there's been a school here before or not,' said Dad more firmly. 'What matters is we've got kids here who need schooling, and we've got a teacher who's prepared to give it to them. I reckon most of you know George Henderson here, or all you from up the gully do anyway. But for those that don't, he was the headmaster at Hastings River for eight years till they

140

closed it down, and a teacher for donkey's years before that. I reckon we couldn't have a better bloke to teach our kids. Anyway, here he is.'

Dad sat down to a burst of clapping, led by his family and taken up gradually by others. Mr Henderson gazed around the hall, and loosened his tie.

'He looks nervous,' muttered Barbara.

'He can't be nervous,' whispered Elaine. 'He's a teacher. He must be used to talking to people.'

'Ladies and gentlemen,' Mr Henderson began formally, 'and residents of the valley.' Then he stopped dead, and cleared his throat. A fly buzzed slowly from one end of the stage to the other and settled on the dusty window.

'Well, go on!' called someone from down below.

'I ...' Mr Henderson's voice seemed to be stuck. He looked helplessly at Dad.

'Never saw a teacher stuck for words before.' It was old man Nicholson's voice again.

'He's not a real teacher,' muttered someone else's voice. 'He's just one of the sussos down Poverty Gully. You can't tell me that if he was a proper teacher he'd be living with that lot down there.'

'Hey! Give the bloke a chance.' Sergeant Ryan rose from his seat. He gazed down at the crowd as though they were a mob of kids caught stealing apples, then turned back to the front. He nodded to Mr Henderson, as though to say, 'Keep going'.

Mr Henderson was silent. He gazed out at the hall. It was as though the last remark had dragged all the words out of him. Barbara gazed up at him, willing him to speak.

'Go on,' whispered Young Jim urgently.

'You can do it, Mr Henderson,' muttered Elaine.

Mr Henderson caught their eyes. He blinked, and then smiled. Suddenly it was as though he was speaking for them, not for himself. He looked out at the audience again, and it was as though he was in the middle of his speech, not at the beginning.

'Some of you may question my qualifications as a teacher,' he said. 'Well, you've every right, seeing where I am now. But it was no fault of mine that led me to Poverty Gully, just as it was no fault of any of the other men and women who live around me. It's the times we live in that brought us here. And if there was any one thing that any of us might have done that might have changed the course of our lives ... well, any failures we've made shouldn't be passed on to the children.

'The children in this valley don't have a school. That means that any future they may have is limited by their lack of education.'

Mr Nicholson snorted, his voice just audible. 'Your education hasn't got you very far, has it?'

Mr Henderson looked at him steadily. 'At least my education gave me the power to choose. A week ago I'd have said I'd made the wrong choices, choices that landed me in a tent in a susso camp. Now I'm not so sure. Because if I can help the kids in this valley get an education, if I can give them the power to choose what they want in their lives, if I can open up the world just a little for them, then I'll know I've made the right choices all along.'

'But how can we have a school?' This voice was bewildered, not antagonistic. 'We don't have a schoolhouse.'

Dad got up again, his trousers settling around his hips.

'We don't need to worry about a schoolhouse. Dulcie here has said we can use her washhouse. Yeah, I know it doesn't look much at the moment, but patch it up a bit, give it a coat of whitewash and I bet we wouldn't call the King our uncle.'

'Who's going to pay for it?' It was Nicholson's voice again. The question was taken up around the hall.

'Yeah, who's going to pay for it?'

'Where's the money coming from?'

'It's the old story all over again,' yelled Mr Nicholson. 'Them that has are supposed to pay for them who hasn't. I worked for my money. I don't see why I should give one brass penny of it to an out-of-work layabout who claims to be a blooming teacher.' There were mutters around the room, some approving, some dismayed. Dad hitched his trousers up again. Someone giggled.

'As for paying the teacher, George here says that maybe the government'll let us have some money. Even if they don't he's willing to give it a burl. He'll work for nothing just to give our kids a chance.'

'Well, what do you want if you don't want money?' someone called.

'All we need is people to help — to fix up the school and to find a place for the Hendersons to live. I had in mind that each of us'd give what we could, even if it's just a couple of rabbits for the pot.'

Mr Henderson looked out over the audience again. 'What we really want,' he said, 'is for you to send us your children. That's what makes a school, the children in it.'

The crowd was silent. It was as if they were waiting for someone else to digest the idea and tell them what to do.

Mr Nicholson cleared his throat in the middle of the room. 'I reckon it's up to the government to give us a school. That's their job. That's what we elect them for.'

'Well they haven't, have they?' said Dad mildly. He frowned, as though trying to put his thoughts into words. 'Those blokes in Sydney are relying on us for their salaries, but instead of them doing what we want, they're doing us down instead. I reckon there's nothing more important than a decent education for our kids. Why should they have to take the crumbs the government throws out to them? I reckon if we want a thing, it's up to us to get it.'

Mr Nicholson stood up slowly. He looked Dad up and down. 'Well, I'll tell you one thing,' he drawled. 'I'm not sending my kids to be taught by a bloke from a susso camp, with a mob of susso urchins in a washhouse.' He looked around the audience for support.

The crowd was quiet. It was impossible to know if they agreed. You could hear the flies bumping at the windows of the hall and the urn hissing down the back. Dad looked helplessly at Mr Henderson. Barbara felt embarrassment shrink her as she sat. Susso urchins, that's all they were.

'Now you just hold it there one minute.' The voice came from the back of the hall. Barbara looked up. It was Gully Jack, leaning against the door jamb. He looked like he hadn't shaved since Friday's dance. He looked like he'd just come from digging in his gully. His shirt hung open where the buttons were gone. The late afternoon sun gleamed behind him, so it was hard to see the expression on his face.

'You just listen to me a minute, Bertie Nicholson. It's all right for you, ain't it, with all your kiddies boarding up in town. They'll get their education, won't they? And how can you afford to send them there? Because of selling rations to the sussos you're so fond of! Where would you be if it weren't for them, I'd like to know? And everyone else who has to buy the maggot-ridden corned beef in your flamin' store.'

'My corned beef has never had maggots in it,' spluttered Mr Nicholson.

Gully Jack looked him up and down. 'Nah,' he agreed. 'The only maggots are in your head. And you know why? Because you can't see that these kids need a chance. That's all you can give anyone in this life. Just a chance. And your fat mouth is taking theirs away.'

Gully Jack looked at the crowd in the hall, craning their necks to look at him. 'Well, what'll it be? Are you going to give these kids a chance or not?'

The crowd was still silent. Mr Nicholson sat down again. He muttered to the men on either side, too low to hear. The silence deepened. Barbara felt her palms grow wet.

Gully Jack stroked his hairy chin pugnaciously. 'Well, is anyone going to speak up or not?'

'I'll give the whitewash.' The voice seemed surprised that it had spoken. 'I mean, I know it's not much. I'll help paint it on too if you can wait till I get the potatoes up.'

'How about roofing iron? Last time I saw that old washhouse it looked like it'd spring a leak any moment. I reckon we've got some left over from the big shed.'

'How about chairs?'

'I can give you half a sheep a week.'

'... a load of wood a week.' That was one of the eucy cutters. 'Struth, they'll need it in the winter there.'

The crowd had woken up now, as though they'd found their feet on the right path and were tearing along it. The offers came from all around the room.

'There's a spare bed up in Olive's room. Would the Hendersons like to use that.'

'If you don't mind eating bunny ...'

Barbara felt tears hot in her eyes, but they were tears of happiness. Young Jim took her hand and held it tight. Elaine was crying too, and trying to sniff without being heard. Ma's face was like the sun had come out behind a cloud and Dad was ecstatic.

There were men crowding around Dad, offering their hands and backs if they had nothing else to give, and Dad was trying to make a list of what everyone was offering. A middle-aged farmer and his wife were talking in low tones to Marge Henderson. 'Well, it's just a shack really, I mean it's nothing much, but I reckon if we had a bit of help we could do it up real nice for you.'

'Guess what?' said Elaine gloomily.

'What?'

'I've changed my mind about my education. You know what all this means? We're going to have to go to school!'

A SCHOOL IN THE WASHHOUSE

'Bubba's tired.'

Barbara wiped the sweat from her forehead, leaving a trail of limey whitewash. 'No I'm not.'

'Yes you are,' insisted Young Jim. He stood back and surveyed their work. The old washhouse gleamed under coats of whitewash. A fresh path of riverstones led to the two new dunnies out the back, carefully lettered 'Girls' and 'Boys', deep holes under rough wooden seats, and there were kero tins of ashes to throw down them to stop the stink and flies. There were faded curtains at the washhouse windows, carefully starched and ironed, and desks and chairs for every child — even though the 'desks' were old tea chests and the 'chairs' were kero tins padded with newspaper and hessian.

The shelves were kero tins as well, rolled on their sides and wired together, filled with books that had been carefully wrapped in newspaper when the Hendersons had moved to the gully, and stored in the tea chest in their tent ever since. Mr. Henderson's desk was the old table from Dulcie's dairy, scrubbed to a pale yellow, but still smelling of slightly sour milk.

Out the front was a blackboard, broken on one side, a reject from the big school up in town. Mr Henderson had persuaded the school to give them their old cracked slates as well, and their worn-out readers with limp covers and mildewed insides. There were old school workbooks, already filled with laborious letters and pothooks and numbers. Marge hoped to erase the ink and pencil marks with lemon juice and stale bread.

She'd put up their poster of the British Empire next to the blackboard, one end discoloured from lying too long in the box in the tent, but the bright pink of the empire was still vivid. There were even dusters and chalk for the blackboard, and new pencils for the slates from the valley store. Gully Jack had gone down to the store and leant on the counter, 'just friendly like', until old man Nicholson had promised to donate them.

'It looks good,' declared Young Jim.

Mr Henderson smiled slightly. He seemed both younger and older than he had a few weeks before, thought Barbara — happier and more approachable, but more like a teacher too.

'It looks like a school,' he said. Elaine made a face.

'When will we start?' asked Barbara.

'How about next Monday?' suggested Mr Henderson. 'Start the week off properly. What do you think?'

'Hip hooray,' muttered Elaine.

Barbara gazed at the gleaming washhouse, at the blue hills behind, fuzzy with autumn light, and the dirt road glowing orange-gold. It seemed strange to think of starting school here, in a washhouse by the creek. But here there'd be no-one to point at her as a foster child, a stranger shuffled from school to school. For the first time she had a family. For the first time there was peace. She smiled suddenly. Paradise in a washhouse, in a susso camp? But it was true.

Jim caught her smile and returned it.

Mr Henderson was still calculating. 'There's the fireplace to finish. That'll take until Friday. Yes, I think we can make it Monday.' He looked at the childen, 'It'd be awfully cold in here in winter if we didn't get a fire going. Your fingers would be too blue to write.'

Winter. Barbara stared at Mr Henderson. That was the other side of paradise. Of course, winter was coming. Already the days were shorter than they'd been a few weeks before and the shadows were longer in the valley in the afternoon. What would the shanty be like in winter? Thellie had had pneumonia last winter, she remembered, and Ma's fingers got crippled with arthritis in the cold. Kids died when the winter winds came. All she'd known with the O'Reillys were the happy days of summer. What would this winter bring them?

The strangeness descended all over again. Dirt floors and hessian sack windows were tolerable in summer. What would it be like to huddle there when the winds blew through the cracks? Even the creek, that sparkling plaything, would be a bitterly cold water source in winter. The gully was a world where there were no antibiotics when you were sick, where people died of a sore tooth, with no electric light or heaters or stoves indoors when it was cold and dark.

She glanced at Elaine and Young Jim. They seemed unconcerned, laughing with Mr Henderson about the bunch of dahlias Mrs Reynolds had sent down to cheer them up while they were working. She'd promised a vase of her best flowers every week, to make the place look cheerful.

Mr Henderson looked at his watch. He'd nearly pawned it when things got bad, but he was glad now that he hadn't. Without a watch, how would they know when to ring the bell?

'Marge'll be expecting me,' he said. 'I promised I'd shift the last of our things over to the MacIntyre's place.' The Hendersons were boarding with the MacIntyres now. Sal, Pat and Gweneth MacIntyre were boarding in town. They'd be able to live at home now there was a school in the valley, and in return the McIntyres had given the Hendersons their back verandah, newly divided into bedroom and living room, with whitewashed hessian walls, and an old slab kitchen out the back to cook their meals in. It was no palace, as Marge said, but a million times better than the tent, and already there was talk of everyone building a schoolmaster's house down in the back corner of Dulcie's bottom paddock.

Mr Henderson smiled at the children. 'See you on Monday,' he told them, 'and thanks for your help. You've worked miracles.'

'How about letting us off the first two weeks homework then?' asked Elaine cheekily.

'No,' said Mr Henderson. He waved to them as he strode off down the track towards the MacIntyres.

Elaine threw the old tussock she'd been using as a whitewash brush into the blackberries. 'Well,' she said. 'What now?'

'A swim,' decided Young Jim. He looked at his whitewash-stained shirt. 'Cripes, if I'd had any sense I'd have taken this off before we started. Skin's easier to clean than shirts.'

'Doesn't wear out either,' added Elaine. 'Come on. Last one in's a dead dog. Hey Bubba, wake up. You look like you're a hundred miles away.'

Jim looked at Barbara in concern. 'What's up Bubba? You feeling all right? You looked beat a little while ago.'

Barbara shook her head. 'I'm fine. I — I just want to think about something. I'll see you at the swimming hole later.'

'You sure you're all right?'

'She's just got too much sense to go swimming in a freezing creek,' said Elaine. 'Leave the girl alone if she wants peace and quiet for a while. Come on, slugfoot. You're as slow as a wet week.'

Barbara thought of the bright green water, the thick shade of the casuarinas, the piercing wind from the tablelands — how much colder would it be swimming in the creek in winter? She tried to smile. 'You go and freeze your toes off. I'll meet you later.'

'Bubba—'

'Oh come on,' interrupted Elaine. 'If we wait any longer we'll cool off and the water'll be murder. Give Bubba some time to herself if she wants it. See you later, Bubba.' Young Jim gave Barbara one last look, then followed his sister up the track.

Barbara watched them go, then walked the other way, up to the hill at the back of Dulcie's. The ground was stony here, the soil too thin for the fat grass the cows liked to munch. Small piles of rabbit dung clung to the tussocks, washed down by last week's rain. Dead leaves curled beneath the trees. A small bird ran up a tree, pecking happily for insects in the bark, then bounced onto a branch and called again, as though boasting of its catch. Barbara climbed to the top of the hill and looked out over the valley.

You could see the police station now, with the police car out the front, and Nicholson's store with its wooden verandah, and the orange twist of road between the dark green verges. You could see Dulcie's house set in its garden of lavender and myrtle and rosemary, and the glint of the creek through the trees. Up the other end was the track that led up to the gully and the drooping fences around Gully Jack's front paddocks.

The paddocks were filling with young wattles, as they returned to bush. Barbara wondered what the farm had been like in his father's day. Had fat, slow cows grazed there, like Dulcie's? Or had they been like Gully Jack himself, restless, dreaming?

It was hard to imagine that only a few weeks ago she'd never even seen the creek — or Gully Jack or Dulcie — or any of the O'Reillys. They'd been so good to her. They'd made this strange world home, the best home she'd ever known. She was one of them. They shared everything they had, but she had nothing at all to give them back, just her silly stories of life around the corner and even they had made Ma sad and Dad's face close up with bitterness.

Ma and Dad were people who gave without thought for themselves. Ma with her scones and comfort, Dad with his restless effort for the school. All the O'Reillys were like that, in their own ways; Elaine, sharp and generous; Young Jim protective of her and all the world.

If only she could give them just some of the things they wanted. Give Thellie an ice-cream, or an aeroplane ride. Help Jim to find his way, find some books for Elaine. If only she could help make winter easier for them. If only she could somehow wave a magic wand and find a house for Ma. If only ...

But she didn't have a magic wand. The only magic she'd ever had was when she walked around the corner. She'd done it once, then she'd tried again and nothing had happened. Should she try it now? What if she woke up somewhere else?

She thought of the draughts threading through the shanty, of Thellie sick and shivering, of Ma with her swollen fingers.

It was worth a try. It was worth trying anything for Ma.

Barbara shut her eyes. There was the corner, just as she'd seen it before. She tried to imagine a house, just around its edge, just out of sight. All she had to do was walk around that corner, and there would be a new house for Ma, with a bathroom and a kitchen stove and soft beds. She imagined herself walking around the corner, but there was no terror moving her, no hands pulling her towards the other side.

A kookaburra cackled. Barbara opened her eyes.

There was no new house.

Despair welled up sharp and sour in her throat. Everything was the same — the dark green paddocks and the wattle regrowth and the faint wisp of smoke coming from the chimney at Gully Jack's house were still there.

Gully Jack's house. An empty house with dusty rooms opening off a faded corridor, a kitchen in which no-one cooked food, except for big slabs of meat.

Could she do it? Did she have the courage? Barbara stood up resolutely. All he could do was say no.

DOWN AT GULLY JACK'S

Rock smelt different in the morning, thought Gully Jack, as he hefted another barrow-load to the channel and carefully began to throw them down on the soft soil so they wouldn't chip.

Afternoon rocks smelt of sunlight, as though they were baby suns themselves, just waiting to hatch. Lunchtime rocks smelt of sweat. Morning rocks still smelt of the soil, cool and sweet, like chocolate from a cold larder. Morning rocks fitted smoothly into your hand and slid into place like they were meant to. It was only later when your hands were numb with tiredness that they began to slip and argue with your fingers and you had to force yourself to keep on going, keep dreaming of the gold hidden in the soil just a few yards — a few months' work — away.

Gold had been a dream as long as he could remember. It had been his dad's dream first. He'd sit at the table while Mum cleared up the dishes after dinner and puff at his pipe, not even noticing that the flame had gone out, and tell him all the stories of the fortune underground; just waiting there for millions of years, his dad had said. Just waiting for them to come and get it out.

When Gully Jack had gone to bed, tucked into clean sheets that his mum had dried on the lavender bushes down the back, tucked in by her hands that still smelt of soap, and mutton fat from tea, he'd dream of the gold too. He could feel it glowing deep under the earth, just waiting for the sun and his hands that would bring it into light. As he got older he could hear it calling, too, a murmur like the creek, but sweeter, a deep clear call from somewhere underground.

His father had talked about gold until his Mum had died, wheezing with the pneumonia. They'd had to harness up the horse early one morning to take her up to the hospital in town. She'd been too sick to see the wattle blossom crowding on the hill. His mum had loved the wattle blossom. He was saddened to think she'd been too sick to notice it when she died. He liked to think she had.

His dad had gone on as usual for a while, milking the cows and sending the milk cans up to town, banking the milk cheque once a month and mending the fences in between the milkings. But his heart wasn't in it. He'd cancelled the order for the new bull from down the coast. The fences were left sagging, while he panned for gold among the casuarina shadows in the creek, until one day he abandoned the milking too, and sold the cows to Dulcie's dad down the valley for a song, and took to panning for the gold full-time.

Gully Jack was still in school then, like Dulcie (she had plaits then, fat as carpet snakes and tied with bright blue ribbons). Dulcie and he boarded through the week in town. His dad let him pan with him on weekends, swirling the muddy water back and forth until the silt and the sand washed away and the tiny sun-bright specks were left. One week he came back to find the pan rusting in the washhouse. He found his dad starting his first channel up the creek.

There wasn't much gold from that one, just a small patch of gold-rich dirt, but there was enough to pay the rates and keep young Jack at school until he was fourteen and he could come home for good.

They started the second channel together, his dad carting the rocks and Jack fitting them in place so the edges wouldn't collapse when they let the water in. Breaking down the last bit of bank between the channel and the creek had been exciting, watching the water eating at the last of the soil, then swirling in brown and hungry as it ate the final barrier, surging up the channel then sweeping back, and washing up again, until there was a calm sweet backwater and they could pan the new seam at the end.

Not that there'd been much gold from that one, or the next. But they'd learnt more about the gold as they went on. Its voice had got clearer in the night. He only had to follow the song of the gold and one day he'd find the seam and see the ancient sunlight flashing in his pan.

The boys he'd been at school with were married now, had farms of their own, or worked in town at the grocer's or the butcher's. The girls had married, too, or gone to teach or nurse or work in other people's kitchens. He'd lost touch with most of them — what was the point of going up to town?

Now and again, late in the afternoon, as the dusk was settling across the gully and it was too dark to work, he'd look at his sagging fences, at the verandah post that was falling down. Or he'd see the wallpaper stains in the lamplight and remember the kitchen in his mother's time, the scents of cheese and stewed apples and baked potatoes and the rumble of the cows outside. He'd imagine for a while what it would be like to have a family of his own. He'd dream of Dulcie, instead of gold, and see her picking chokoes from the vine that grew across the dunny.

Perhaps, when he found the gold. There wouldn't be any need to pick the chokoes then. They could buy their vegies down at the store. They could go up to Sydney or holiday at the beach and Dulcie would be dressed in silk and ermine. The dream would fade a little there, at the thought of the holidays in Sydney, at the beach, the empty places in his life, with no more gold to dig, no more rocks to place along his channels, no more dreams of sunlight underground. He'd work just a little slower the next day, so as not to get the gold too fast, to keep his dream alive. By the next day the worry would be forgotten and the sweat would trickle down his neck again as he worked from kookaburra-dawning until the dark.

Gully Jack looked down at his pile of rocks, satisfied. It was a good pile now. Enough to keep him going all afternoon. He was about to jump down into the channel when he heard a kookaburra call a warning. He looked up.

'Hello. Bubba, isn't it? Where're the others?'

'Jim and Elaine are down at the creek. The others are up home, I suppose.'

The kid looked nervous, as though there was a mad dog about to bite. Gully Jack smiled, to try and make her feel better. 'What's on your mind?'

Barbara sat cautiously on a large rock, spreading her skirts around her knees. She looked like she was trying to work out what to say. 'It's about your house.'

'My house? What's wrong with my house?'

'Nothing. Nothing at all. It's just it's so big, and there's just you in it, and you were saying the other day that you wished you had someone to cook for you and all.'

Gully Jack thought of Dulcie, holding his cup of tea for him at the hall, remembered her smiling at Sergeant Ryan. He forced his mind back.

'I suppose I might have. So what?'

'Well, I was wondering if maybe the O'Reillys could live with you. I mean Ma could do your cooking and Dad could repair the house. The verandah looks like it's going to fall down any day and one of the stumps under the kitchen looked rotten, I couldn't help seeing ...' Barbara's words came out in a rush. 'And Dad could grow his vegies in one of the paddocks. I mean, it'd give you more time to work here if you didn't have to cook or weed your vegies, and he's really good at growing vegies. Maybe he could sell them and then he could pay you rent.'

Gully Jack sat stunned. What an idea — sharing his house with another family, seeing Ma O'Reilly in his mum's kitchen, with those kids running through all the rooms. But they were good kids. It was a pleasure to hear them laugh and it wouldn't be as though they'd bother him much, as he was never in. And Bubba was right — O'Reilly could fix up the place. It wasn't right to let it go, but what else could he do, the channel took up all his time.

Barbara had taken his silence for anger. She stood. 'Look, I'm sorry to have bothered you. It was just an idea.'

Gully Jack held up a hand. 'No. Stop. It's not a bad idea. It just needs thinking about. I mean it's not something you can jump up and yell "Yes" to, is it? I mean a bloke's got to think about something as serious as this.'

Barbara sat down again. Gully Jack looked at her. 'Dulcie was telling me you think you're from the future. She says you just walked around a corner and you were here.' Barbara nodded. Gully Jack shook his head. 'Struth girl, couldn't you have chosen a better corner to walk around than this? Smack bang into a susso camp and living in a shack.'

'It's not so bad.' She lifted her chin. 'The O'Reillys have been good to me. They're wonderful people.'

'So you want to do something for them in return,' said Gully Jack shrewdly. 'If they can't walk around the corner for themselves you'll fix it for them like they have.' Gully Jack gazed down at the smooth rocks in his gully. For a moment they blurred and he almost saw around the corner too. There was a gully and another seam of gold at the end of it, but this time there was a good dinner at the close of the day, and company around the table, the kids laughing in the raspberries at the bottom of the garden.

'You're on,' he said suddenly.

The girl blinked. 'I beg your pardon?'

'I said you're on. You tell the O'Reillys they can move down any time they like. I'll sharefarm with O'Reilly if he wants to. You know what sharefarming is?'

Barbara shook her head.

'Well, he does the work, but it's my farm. If he can make any money out of those vegies of his we share it, so much for him and so much for me. Struth, if he does any good at it I'll sell him a paddock or two, but we'll think about that later. All right?'

Barbara's face glowed like gold. 'All right!' She thought for a minute. 'Will you tell them, or will I?'

Gully Jack grinned. 'It was your idea. You should have the glory.'

'No,' she decided. 'You tell them. Let them think it was your idea. Is that okay with you?'

'It's all right with me,' said Gully Jack slowly. 'I just think you should have the credit too. But if that's the way you want it, okay.'

'It's the best way.' Barbara stood up to go, then came to him quickly and kissed his prickly cheek. 'You'll never be sorry,' she promised. 'Never.'

Gully Jack watched her running up the track, her skirt flashing through the trees. The world felt different suddenly, as if he'd gone around a corner, just like she had. It felt different. That was all.

BUNYAS

It was hot down at the creek. The still air was full of sweat and eucalyptus oil.

Elaine and Young Jim sprawled in the casuarina shade after their swim and let the hot air wash over their cooled bodies.

'Do you think Bubba's all right? She was awfully quiet this morning.'

'Don't tie yourself in knots,' said Elaine lazily. She tossed a pebble into the creek, trying to make it skim across the water. It made a rude noise, and sank. 'She must just find things a bit strange, that's all. I mean wherever she came from, it's got to be a heck of a lot different from this.'

'I suppose,' said Young Jim. He pulled his carving out of his pocket and began to scrape at it slowly with his knife. 'I just wish I could've taken her somewhere halfway decent. I mean a place with a proper house and everything. Struth, I wish I could give every kid in Australia a proper house, and decent tucker.'

'Get off your soapbox, will you,' ordered Elaine drowsily. 'You can't change the world yourself. Not all of it at once, at any rate.' She yawned. 'We'll need another swim soon. I've never known it so sultry.' Elaine rested her head on her arms. She shut her eyes, then opened them.

'I should think things were changing round here fast enough even for you,' she said.

'What's up with you?' Young Jim looked up from his carving at the sudden seriousness of her voice.

Elaine shrugged, her face down in the casuarina needles again. 'Just the thought of school, I suppose.'

'I thought you wanted an education.'

''Course I want an education. I just don't want to go to school. I wish someone would invent a sort of education medicine — you know, you take a teaspoon every morning and it teaches you everything you wanted to know. Then you could spend the rest of the day like this, swimming and ... and just wandering round the world.'

Young Jim snorted. 'If wishes were fishes we'd all be rich. You've got to work for what you want in this world, kiddo. You don't get things handed to you on a plate.'

'It's all right for you.' Elaine sat up and searched for another flat pebble among the flood debris on the bank. 'You'll be fourteen in a few weeks, old enough to leave school if you want to. You'll be free of school forever.'

'Maybe not.' Jim turned the carving in his hand, trying to judge its shape.

He had carved a lizard this time, a miniature dragon like the ones in the creek, with a high inquisitive head and leathery folds around its throat.

'What do you mean?'

'I've been thinking I might keep trying for my Intermediate. Maybe even get my Leaving.'

'How's that going to help you change the world?' demanded Elaine unkindly.

'Dunno. But I reckon you've got to know a bit about the

163

world before you change it. Who knows, maybe I'll even get to the university one day.'

'Where'd you get the money?'

Young Jim grinned suddenly. 'Let's just say I can see it round the corner.'

Elaine snorted. 'You've been listening to Bubba. Everyone's been listening to Bubba. You've all gone crazy.'

'Why not? What's wrong with dreaming? If she can have a place round the corner why can't I?'

'Except her corner's different. She didn't want to come here. Did you Bubba?'

Young Jim started. He hadn't seen Barbara walk up. She looked different somehow. Her face was glowing like starlight through the trees. She looked like she was hugging a secret and wouldn't let it go. She poked him with her toe, then made herself comfortable on the casuarina needles. 'Lazybones. You look like a mob of lizards soaking up the sun.'

Elaine scratched at a mosquito bite on her leg.

'Just enjoying our freedom while we can,' she said philosophically.

'Too right,' agreed Young Jim. He slipped his penknife into his pocket. 'I'm going up the gully to look for bunyas. It's probably the last chance we'll get before Monday. Anyone else coming?'

'Not me,' said Elaine. 'That's a mug's game.'

'What's a bunya?' asked Barbara.

Young Jim laughed. 'Come on then, I'll show you.'

Elaine stood up and shook the bark and leaves off her skirt. 'I wouldn't if I were you,' she informed her. 'Even getting wood with the littl'uns is better than getting bunyas.'

'You'll be sorry when we bring them home,' threatened Young Jim. 'If you don't hunt them you can't eat them.'

Elaine snorted. 'I didn't say I wouldn't eat them. You find them and I'll cook them. Fair exchange. I'll even bring the water up for Ma instead of you.'

'Fair enough.' Young Jim grinned. 'Come on, Bubba, before she changes her mind. I'll sneak home and get some sacks and then we're off.'

It was dark underneath the tree. It smelt musty and felt prickly on her feet. Barbara craned upward, trying to see Young Jim through the branches.

'Look out below!'

It sounded like a bomb was crashing through the tree, landing with a thud of broken branches and dusty leaves on the other side. Barbara ran to look at it.

'It's huge!' she yelled up to Young Jim.

'Told you so!' Young Jim sounded hot and breathless. 'Stand clear. There's another one just here.'

'You be careful!' yelled Barbara.

'Go teach your grandmother to suck eggs! I've done this dozens of times. You just make sure you keep out of the way. If you get one of these on your head you'll be flatter than a pancake. Here it comes!'

'I'll just find one more. *Ouch!*'

'What's wrong?'

'Cripes! It's these blasted prickles. I got one in my bum. Hey, don't you laugh, it hurts.'

'Well I'm not going to kiss it better, *that's* for sure.' Barbara poked her toe at the giant balls by her feet. 'How are we going to get these home anyway?'

'That's what I brought the sacks for. You carry one nut and I'll put the other two in mine. Think you can manage it?'

'If you can carry two I can carry one,' said Barbara with determination.

'Huh, listen to her. They'll make you a strong man in the circus next.'

'Nah, I'll just stick you in a cage and call you a gorilla and charge five dollars admission.'

'Five what?' Young Jim's head peered down through the branches.

'Dollars. Oh! Like pounds — you know, money, cash.'

'Sure I know what dollars are. Yanks have them. You have dollars too, where you come from?'

'Sure. Since — I'm not sure — in the sixties sometime.'

Young Jim laughed high up in his tree. 'Crazy, crazy, crazy. Think anyone'd really pay five quid to see my face?'

'Nah. Tuppence ha'penny maybe and even then they'd want their money back. You've got a face like the back end of a budgie.'

'Garn! Where'd you hear that one?'

'Gully Jack. He said Mrs Reynolds has got a face like the back end of a budgie and she plays the piano like a cockatoo with chilblains. All because she said his fiddle was out of tune at last Friday's dance.'

Young Jim laughed. 'Maybe I should sing then. You think people might pay to hear me sing?' He began yelling at the top of his voice:

'Hallelujah I'm a bum,
Hallelujah bum again.'

'Hey, that's the song that kid was singing!'

'Well, I can sing it too, can't I? I bet my voice is better than his ...

> *Oh, people say bum,*
> *Save the money you earn,*
> *Well if I didn't eat I'd have money to burn,*
> *Hallelujah I'm a bum—'*

'Well, it's louder anyway,' commented Barbara.
'Spoilsport. Come on ...

> *Hallelujah bum again,*
> *Hallelujah show us your garters, to revive us again.*
> *Oh why don't you work, like other men do?*
> *Well how can I work when the sky is so blue*

... Just like Gully Jack isn't it? Can you imagine him all shut up in an office?

> *Hallelujah I'm a bum,*
> *Hallelujah bum again,*
> *Hallelujah show us your garters,*

— Barbara joined in —

> *To revive us again.*
> *I went to the door,*
> *To ask for some bread,*
> *But the lady said bum bum*
> *the baker is dead,*
> *Hallelujah I'm a bum*

... Hey, what's up?'

'Just got a bit of leaf in my throat,' complained Barbara.

'You going to stay up there all day singing, or what?'

'Nearly got it.' Young Jim sawed carefully with his pocketknife. 'All clear below?'

'All clear!' The final nut landed near the others. There was a shower of dead leaves and bits of bark as Young Jim made his way carefully down the bunya tree, avoiding the sharp leaves as best he could, hunting out footholds in the rough bark.

'Cripes, I'm glad I borrowed Dad's old long pants. My legs'd be cut to ribbons.'

'Just as long as you don't tear his pants.'

'He'd forgive me, as long as I brought the bunyas home.'

'I wouldn't bet on it.' Barbara gave one of the giant nuts a shove with her toe. 'Sure you can eat these things?'

'Sure I'm sure. I've brought them back dozens of times. You just throw them in the fire till they open and the nuts are cooked. You've never eaten anything till you've eaten bunya nuts.'

'I've never heard of them,' admitted Barbara.

'Don't they have bunya trees where you come from?'

'Don't think so.'

Young Jim began to stuff the giant nuts in the sacks. He seemed to be thinking. Finally he looked back up at Barbara.

'Bubba, I was wondering. Would you go back now if you could?'

'Go where?'

'Back home.'

Barbara's face shut cold and tight. 'I don't have a home.'

'Of course you do, silly. Your home is here. You know what I mean — back to your own time.'

Barbara hesitated. 'I don't know. No. No, I wouldn't. I tried when I first came here. I didn't tell you, because you'd all been so kind. I sat down by the creek and tried to think myself around the corner.'

'What happened?'

'It didn't work. Maybe I just didn't try hard enough. I didn't really want to get back.'

'What about now?'

'Now I want to stay here. This is home, like you said.'

Young Jim didn't say anything. He just grinned, slowly and happily, and nodded. He went back to stuffing the nuts into the sacks.

'Here,' he said. 'Think you can lift it?'

'Sure.' Barbara heaved it over her shoulder. It was heavier than she'd expected and awkward, bobbing around and hitting the back of her legs with every step. 'I think I can manage it.'

'Good girl.' Young Jim hoisted his own. His knees bent under the strain, bulging like grapefruits. 'We'd better get a move on then. I don't like the look of the sky.' He pointed towards the end of the valley. The clouds were massed like bright purple marshmallows, tinged with green.

'Think there'll be a storm?'

'I reckon. Should have guessed there'd be one after the heat this morning. Looks like it's moving up this way. I haven't seen clouds like that since the first week we were in the valley. Dad'd only just got the vegie bed dug and the rain washed all the soil away. Came down in sheets.' He peered at the sky again. 'It's getting darker. Come on, shift your tail.'

It was hard walking with a sack of bunya nut. The sun

poured through the trees, ignoring the fat clouds at the end of the valley. The sweat made little gullies down Barbara's face and neck. She should have worn a hat, she thought, except she didn't have one. None of the O'Reillys seemed to wear hats, except when they were dressed up. Dad had worn a felt hat to the meeting, and Ma had worn a hat too, a funny one that only covered half her head with a bit of netting on the side, nothing that would keep the sun off. No-one here had ever heard of the greenhouse effect and the thinning ozone layer. Maybe they'd never even heard of skin cancer. Perhaps she should make a hat. If you could make your own house and school and furniture surely you could make a hat. She could make everyone hats for Christmas presents.

The air felt wet already, too thick with humidity to push through. Barbara let her sack fall and tried to catch her breath. Young Jim shook his head.

'Come on. We've got to get going. Look!'

The world was darker, almost shadowless. The sky was a dull, smooth grey above their heads and blackish-purple above the ridges. The air smelt like burnt electrical cord. A pair of currawongs darted towards shelter, their wings flapping heavily in the thick air. Thunder grumbled somewhere beyond the horizon.

They'd reached the creek when the rain began. Suddenly the air turned liquid, each drop so hard it stung their faces.

'Drop the sack!' yelled Young Jim.

'What about the nuts?'

'They won't melt. We'll pick them up later. We'll drown if we stay out in this!'

They battled through the heavy air. Barbara tried to push her hair out of her eyes, but the rain thrust it back again. Her skirt clung to her legs as though it was trying to tie them together.

Ma was looking for them, standing outside the shack, a newspaper held above her head to shield her from the spray as the rain danced on the tin. She began to scold as soon as they were near.

'No more sense than a pair of chickens! You'd think you were both old enough now to know when to come in out of the rain. And look at your Dad's good trousers. Bubba, you get out of those wet things, there's dry clothes out for you on the bed. You get that hair dry too. Young Jim, I don't want to hear another word out of you till you're dry. What were you thinking of, keeping Bubba out in the rain like that. There's stew still hot in the camp oven, not that you deserve a drop of it.'

It was warm inside the shack, a smelly friendly warmth from lots of bodies. The little ones were on Ma's bed, lifting up the canvas window so they could see the rain. Elaine handed Barbara the dry clothes — a skirt that looked as if it had been one of Dulcie's, long and faded, and a jumper that might have come from Dulcie's father, mended at the elbows, slightly frayed around the neck. It smelt of lavender and cloves, prickly, warm and dry.

Elaine watched her dress. 'It's all right, she's decent,' she yelled to Young Jim. 'You can come in now. Here, Joey, you stick some newspaper in her shoes will you? They're absolutely sodden.' She shook her head. 'You should've heard Ma when you weren't back. She was afraid the creek'd flood and you'd be trapped on the other side.'

'Do you think it'll flood?'

'Shouldn't be surprised,' said Young Jim, towelling his hair with a bit of sacking as he came in the door. He was in dry clothes too, the cut-off trousers Barbara had first seen him in and the same blue faded shirt. It seemed so long ago now, as though Poverty Gully was the only real world there'd ever been.

Young Jim knelt on the bed next to Thellie. 'Look at that rain,' he marvelled. 'You'd think someone had turned on all the taps in heaven.' He looked around. 'Where's Dad?'

'Down at the school.' Ma bustled in, a plate of stew in either hand. 'You get this into you before you catch your death of cold. There's more if you want it. Sergeant Ryan brought up some old tin from down the Valley. Mr Henderson thought a verandah out the front would be a good idea. You can eat your lunches there when it rains.'

'I suppose he brought it up in the police car.'

'What if he did?'

'I'd like to hear what Sydney'd say if they knew about it.'

'What Sydney doesn't know won't hurt them. Sergeant Ryan keeps better order in this valley than the lot of them up there with their batons and arrests.'

'That's right, you tell them Ma.'

'And none of your lip either,' said Ma. 'Or I'll be making some arrests of my own.' She looked up at the ceiling where a large fat drop of water was gathering. 'If there's any tin left over we could do with a few repairs. What I wouldn't do to have a proper roof over us by winter.'

Barbara smiled to herself. She wondered when Gully Jack would come up. After dinner, probably. She couldn't wait to see Ma's face, and Dad's.

Thellie edged over to Barbara and peered at her stew. 'You still hungry?' asked Barbara.

Thellie took her thumb out of her mouth. 'No. Ma made me eat all my pumpkin. My tummy says it'll burst if you stick a pin in it. I want a story. Will you tell me a story, Bubba?'

Barbara looked at her, her face still smeared with stew, her big eyes clear and happy. It was funny the way her old life was just a story to amuse the kids now. It was so far away it almost didn't hurt at all any more.

'Okay. What'll I tell you? Hey, do you know about Big Macs, and pizzas, and video games, and—'

She talked between spoonfuls of stew, while the water thundered on the roof and slid down the sides of the shack. Young Jim sat whittling in his corner, smiling to himself as she talked. She put her empty plate down and Thellie curled up on the bed beside her. The other little ones curled up too, and the stories of her past life entertained them as it rained.

'And the cars make so much noise it's like an ocean, always roaring, and there are no horses on the streets at all.'

'Not even pulling the baker's van?'

'Not even the baker's van.'

'Or the milkman's either?'

'Or the milkman's.'

'Where do you get the manure for your gardens then?'

Barbara was nonplussed. 'Oh, I suppose people just buy fertiliser from the garden centre, or the supermarket.'

'What's a supermarket?'

Thellie could have been asking about fairy palaces, or dragons with scales like rainbow-coloured armour.

'It's a great big shop, a hundred times as big as Nicholson's, with everything on shelves. You just walk down with a trolley and pick up what you want.'

Thellie bounced up and down.

'And you don't have to pay?'

'Of course you have to pay, but not till you get to the checkout — that's when you want to leave the shop. Not like down the valley where you have to ask the man behind the counter for the things you want.'

'Can you get ice-cream in the super things?' asked Thellie dreamily.

'Of course. There's whole freezers full of ice-cream, great big buckets of it, all different sorts, and frozen yoghurt and ice-cream cake and sorbet and ...'

'I've had three ice-creams,' said Joey importantly. 'One on my birthday two years ago, and one from the machine at the railway station when we came down here, and—'

'I've had an ice-cream too,' broke in Thellie.

'Not as many as me you haven't,' said Joey.

'Have so too. I've had—'

'Finished,' exclaimed Young Jim. He held up his carving so it caught the light. The lizard's eyes were shut and its mouth was open. Its forelegs were long and straight and its tail curled around toward its head. Young Jim brushed the wood chips off his lap.

'What do you think of it?' He tossed it over to Barbara.

She ran a finger over it. 'It's beautiful. Look at its eyes and everything, and the way its skin folds under its chin. It's exactly like the dragons down on the rocks.'

'You keep it then,' said Young Jim.

'Can I really? But—'

'Just rub a bit of dripping into it to stop any cracking,' ordered Young Jim. 'And don't you let it get wet, mind, or leave it out in the sun.'

'Hey, the rain's stopping,' said Joey. 'Look.'

Barbara knelt on the bed and peered out the window. The rain had gentled to a thin, wet, mist. Fat clouds hung over the ridges, round as Dulcie's scones. The first streaks of sunset lit the horizon, grey then pink, and gold below.

'Almost like it's morning just over the horizon,' said Young Jim.

'I suppose it's always morning somewhere,' said Elaine. 'Come on, let's go and see the creek. There'll be a flood for sure!'

FLOOD!

The air smelt clean, like freshly washed socks. Diamond raindrops shimmered in the casuarinas, and the bark of the gum trees shone cream and orange.

The kids raced down the hill, their bare feet pressing the wet dirt and grass.

'Hey look, it's not up yet.'

'Won't be long!' yelled Young Jim. 'Listen!'

There was a rumbling up the gorge as a wall of water swept around the bend.

The clear creek water was smothered by the flood, sucked under by the raging silt and mud and water. Boulders ground together like giant teeth as they rolled over and over under the swirling foam. The ground shuddered beneath their bare feet.

'It's frightening,' whispered Barbara. 'Everything so calm and peaceful then suddenly this comes from round the bend.'

'Can't hear you!' yelled Young Jim over the noise of the water. 'No you don't, Joey. You keep away from the edge.'

'I won't fall in,' said Joey indignantly.

'Says who?' Young Jim grabbed his hand.

'Where's Thellie?' demanded Elaine. 'Blast the kid, there she is over there. She's heading for Gully Jack's channel.'

'Probably wants to see if it's flooded too,' said Young Jim. 'Thellie! You come back here! Thellie!'

'She can't hear above the flood,' said Barbara. 'I'll go and bring her back.'

'Don't be long!' Elaine called after her. 'It'll be pitch dark soon.'

The grass along the creek bank was slippery, dark green and pointing upwards like it had drunk deep. The whole gully had changed. The groan of the water smothered the song of wind and leaves; the smell of the flood not the scent of bark and bush. The trees glowed as the light of dusk filtered through the raindrops on the leaves.

'Thellie! Thellie, come back here.' Barbara tried to yell above the noise of the water.

Thellie looked up. She was standing by Gully Jack's channel. The channel was empty, although the creek lashed high and furious beyond the wall at the end. Already the waves were eating at the remaining dirt, tearing into it and gradually swirling it away. Thellie shook her head as Barbara beckoned and pointed down.

'What is it?'

Thellie's eyes were wide. 'Is that gold?' she asked.

Barbara looked down into the channel. Part of Gully Jack's stonework had collapsed. A pile of rocks lay tumbled in wet mud and one of them had cracked in two. She could see dark grey specks and bright white quartz, and in the centre a ring of dull yellow.

'It can't be gold. Things like that don't happen.'

'I think it's gold,' said Thellie with certainty.

'Maybe you're right. It's got to be gold, nothing else would gleam like that. A nugget in the rock. Oh, wow,

wow!' Barbara shook her head in disbelief. 'Gully Jack's found gold and he doesn't even know it.'

'We could take it to him!' Thellie sat on the muddy bank as though she was going to wriggle down.

'No way. You stay just where you are.' Barbara peered down at the mud and rock below. 'It's dangerous. That channel's going to flood any moment. We'll have to get him and see if he can ... Thellie, no!'

The ground was moving. Sodden with water, the bank under their feet was slowly collapsing. Barbara flung herself back as her feet tried to follow the subsiding soil.

'Thellie! Are you all right?' She clambered back to the edge of the channel on her hands and knees. 'Thellie!'

'Bubba, I fell.' Thellie's voice was frightened. Her face was small and white as she peered up.

'Did you hurt yourself?'

'I banged my knee.'

'Is that all? Well, you get up here now. It's not safe.'

'I can't. It's too far up.'

'Heck!' Barbara lay down on her stomach and stretched out her hand. 'Come on, I'll pull you up. Can you grab hold of my hand?'

Thellie stretched, standing on tiptoe. 'I can't reach.'

'Well, climb up then. Come on, it's not far, and then I'll grab you.'

Thellie thrust one small bare foot into the mud. She tried to wedge her fingers into the dampness up above. Her foot slipped as the sodden clay collapsed again.

'Bubba, it won't stay still.'

'Well, stand on a rock or something.' Barbara looked around frantically. They needed a rope, or someone with longer arms to pull the child out, but she couldn't leave Thellie like this to get help, not with the flood and the darkness. There was nothing else for it.

'I'm coming down,' she called, 'Look out.' She aimed for a clear spot below, and jumped.

The shock of it jarred her. Mud squelched through her toes, around her ankles.

'Okay, you get on my shoulders and I'll heave you out. All right?' Barbara tried to get close to the bank, but the fallen rocks and slipping mud were in the way. 'We've got to hurry. Up you go. One, two, three — now grab on to the bank and heave.'

'I can't.' Thellie was nearly crying. 'It's still too far up.'

Barbara bent down so Thellie could climb off her shoulders. She put her arm around her, one eye on the foam that swirled above the muddy wall at the end of the channel. Thellie was shivering. 'It's all right Thellie. It's all right. We'll get out somehow.' She glanced at the wall at the end of the channel again. Was that water trickling through?

'Bubba! What's happened?'

'Jim, and Elaine. Thank heavens. Thellie fell and I can't get her out.'

Young Jim's face was grim. He'd seen the trickle of water at the end of the channel too. 'Heave her up, then I'll have a go. Thellie, reach out towards me. Hurry, blast it, hurry! Bubba, can't you get any closer?'

Barbara shook her head frantically. 'The bank just keeps collapsing.'

'Struth! It's no good. This flaming edge's collapsing even more. Elaine, get Gully Jack. Hurry! Tell him to grab some rope. Run! That wall's going to go soon.' He bent down to the channel again, careful not to get too close in case more soil and rock hurtled down below. 'Are you sure you can't climb up?'

Barbara shook her head desperately. How much time did they have before the water flooded in? 'All the stones are loose, and the walls just collapse when we put any weight on them.'

'Can't you climb up on one? Look, I'll see if I can roll a boulder down. Maybe if you or Thellie stand on that.'

'No!'

'What is it?'

'Don't go away. I'm scared. Please stay till Elaine gets back.'

'Bubba, it'll be all right.' Young Jim looked desperately at the end of the channel. The trickle of water was eating the mud away as it came through in a stready stream. The floodwaters must be tearing at the other side.

'Don't leave us.'

'Of course I won't leave. I'll always look after you. I've just got to ... oh, here they come. Gully Jack, over here! Hurry!' Young Jim's voice was high with relief.

Gully Jack's whiskery face appeared over the edge of the channel. His hands looked big and hard and capable.

'You all right down there? You just hold on then and she'll be right.' His face disappeared, but his voice floated down, calm and reassuring. 'I'm just tying the rope to this tree.' His face came back, framed by the anxious faces of Young Jim and Elaine.

'Right. Now you grab it as it comes down. That's the girl ... now tie it around Thellie's waist, as fast as you can, but don't fumble it. That's the ticket ... good. Now lift her up as far as you can. You get the other end, Young Jim. Elaine, you grab it too. Now haul her up. Carefully now.'

Thellie rose slowly up, out of the channel. The mud grasped at her, trying to suck her in, but the hands above were too strong. She disappeared over the edge.

Barbara was alone. She leant against the wet wall, waiting for the rope to fall again, almost sobbing with relief. It was going to be okay. She could just see Gully Jack above her, quickly untying the rope from Thellie.

'Gully Jack! Hurry! It's going!' It was Young Jim's voice, choked and desperate.

Barbara turned. The wall at the end of the channel had vanished. In its place was a wall of water, higher than her head, brown and frothy, crashing down the channel towards her. She could smell it; the stink of flood had taken over the world. She could feel it; a deep vibration through the earth and air.

Time seemed to change and the world slowed suddenly. The terror was slowed too, seeping through her feet, her legs, her arms. Even if the rope came down now she couldn't reach for it, she couldn't move. Terror held her still. Faintly, through the fear, she heard Young Jim above her, his arms stretched uselessly towards her. 'Bubba ... Bubba ... hang on.'

His voice altered. She heard another voice, an older voice, but somehow still the same. *'Things are different around the corner ... around the corner you'll be safe.'*

She could feel the thunder of the water through her feet. It crashed and bit towards her, but it moved so slowly ... everything was slow. Would it take her slowly too ... churn her slowly under foam and froth, crash her slowly against the grinding boulders? It couldn't be happening, not like this. She had to run ... she had to move ... but there was only one way she could go now.

'Bubba!' Young Jim's voice was despairing.

Barbara shut her eyes.

BACK AROUND THE CORNER

The water grabbed her, tore her, whirled her deep inside. It battered her, sucked at her and tossed her about. She wanted to scream; she wanted to breathe; she waited for the flood to fill her mouth, her eyes, her lungs, but it wasn't water, it was something else.

It was the chaos that had taken her before, but that time she'd been in control, that time she'd had the corner clear inside her mind. She had to find the corner, the corner at the edge of her mind. She tried to clear her mind, but it was filled with molten colours, shapes, sounds and all the ways the world could turn were twisting in her head ... it must be there ... it must ...

Suddenly it was clear again. All she had to do was walk, but her feet were lost inside the whirlpool. She couldn't find them, couldn't move. How had she moved before? She'd used the strength of terror, she'd harnessed it to her feet. She could feel them now, she could lift them, oh so slowly, the corner was getting closer, nearer all the time.

Before there had been hands to help her. There were no hands now, although something was pulling her. She recognised it amid the chaos. It was her world, the reality she'd always known was waiting for her, pulling her, taking her back.

What would she find around the corner now? The demonstration where it all began? The screams, the pain at home. The Gully was home, with Jim and Ma, the family ... one more step and she'd be around ... somewhere safe around the corner.

The whirlpool slowed. There were colours again, greens and blues. There were sounds that she could almost hear. One more step and she'd be free of the confusion.

The world was quiet.

Then ... she heard a bird singing; the creek muttering nearby. A child laughed and called to someone.

Barbara opened her eyes. The trees were the same, the high dark casaurinas, but these were dusted with pollen, not the sparkle of rain. The sky was a deep clear blue, without a trace of cloud.

Barbara sat up. Her bones ached. There was mud on her arms, her legs. Her skirt was caked with mud. Dulcie's skirt ... where was Dulcie, and Ma, Young Jim, and Thellie ...

She looked around. The grass along the creek was roughly mown. The trees were sparse, just the casuarinas left along the creek and a few among the swings and seesaws. Beyond the nearest trees she could see the high fence of a tennis court, with brick barbecues beyond, and a block of toilets at the far end of the porch.

There was no-one near. The child's voice came again, beyond the tennis court.

It was real, but she couldn't let it be real. She wanted to go back to the time before. Somewhere around the corner.

All she had to do was go back around the corner. She shut her eyes, and tried to visualise the corner. The bright sunlight turned her eyelids red. She couldn't concentrate. No matter how hard she tried it wasn't there. She shut her eyes tighter. It had to be there. But there was no terror, no hands pulling her that final step. This was her world. There was nowhere else to go.

She opened her eyes and tried to stand up. Her legs were wobbly. What should she do now? Where should she go? Her mind felt thick, as thick as her tongue.

They were gone. Thellie, the little ones, Ma and Dad and Elaine. Gully Jack was gone, and Dulcie and Young Jim, who'd said that he'd always look after her, he'd always be there, but he was gone as well. Under the hurt and weariness, she felt no surprise. She'd always known, without ever really thinking about it, that her time in the gully was borrowed. She remembered Dad saying he was going to make his own world around the corner, a world for his kids to learn in. She had to make her own world around the corner now. If she could.

Barbara looked down at her skirt. She had to wash. Wherever she was going, she couldn't go like this. She looked down at the creek. It was clear and smiling, glittering between its stones, as though it had never roared and thrust and snatched.

It was strangely difficult to climb down to the water. Her body knew of the danger now. But nothing happened when she touched the surface. It was simply clear and cold and wet. She waded further out and began to wash her legs and arms, to ease the mud from between her toes, to scrub the worst of the mud stains from the skirt.

A giggle interrupted her. She looked up. There was a child on the bank; a girl with thin blonde hair and dark wide eyes. Her smile was as bright as the sun.

'Thellie!'

The child blinked. 'My name's not Thellie,' she informed her. She looked down curiously. 'What're you doing? How did you get so muddy?'

'In the gully ...' Barbara faltered. There was no gully now. It must have been filled in years before and grass had covered it. There was no mud at all.

'If I got as muddy as that I wouldn't be allowed to watch TV,' confided the child. 'Why are you washing in the creek? Mummy says it's too cold to swim in the creek now. Why don't you go home and use the bathroom?'

'I haven't got a bathroom,' said Barbara in confusion. She wondered if she should ask what year it was. But the child was probably too young to know and there was no need. It was her time, 1994.

The child considered. 'You can use our bathroom,' she offered. 'We've got two bathrooms now. We got a new one last year. The new one's got red tiles and ...' She looked around as a tall woman came in sight. 'Mum, can this girl use our bathroom because she's muddy and she hasn't got a bathroom of her own.'

The woman cast a worried look at Barbara. Barbara could guess what she saw: a strange girl, white-faced and filthy, in a ragged skirt with bare feet and mud-streaked hair.

'Of course she has a bathroom,' said the woman. 'Everyone has a bathroom. Come on now, we'll be late for lunch. Granny's waiting.'

'But what about the girl?'

The child was insistent, sensing there was more trouble than a dirty skirt.

'The girl will be all right.' The woman hesitated as she looked down again. 'You are all right, aren't you?' she asked.

Barbara shook her head. She didn't know what to say, how to explain.

The woman stood, thinking, then came over to the bank. She wore jeans and leather sandals. Her hair was cut fashionably around her face.

'Are you lost? You're not from round here, are you? Where's your home?'

'I haven't got a home.'

The words faded as she spoke them. She *did* have a home, they'd promised her she did; home was with the O'Reillys.

Something was digging into her leg. Something in her pocket. She fished it out. It was the lizard, the tiny wooden water dragon that Young Jim had carved and given her a few hours, and sixty years, ago! She stroked it, remembering. He'd promised her, hadn't he? It was crazy to hope but there was still one last chance.

The woman was impatient. 'Are you visiting someone here then?'

Barbara tried to think. If only her mind wasn't so tired.

'Young Jim,' she said slowly, feeling the dragon warm in her palm. 'Young Jim O'Reilly.'

She expected the woman not to know who she was talking about. It was impossible Young Jim should still be here, surely. But the woman seemed to be considering. She looked Barbara up and down again.

'You're looking for Jim O'Reilly?' she asked. 'Do you know him, or do you just want to talk to him?'

'I'm a friend,' said Barbara firmly. She was sure at least of that.

The woman was hesitant still. 'Jim O'Reilly lives in Sydney now,' she said slowly.

Would he remember her? He was the only link with security she had. 'Could you give me his address? His phone number?'

'It's in the book,' said the woman dismissively. She seemed about to go. The child tugged her skirt. The woman seemed to reconsider. She turned back to Barbara.

'You won't find him at home though,' she admitted. 'He had an accident three weeks ago.'

'An accident—'

'He broke his hip. He's in Eastcliff Private Hospital.'

The child squatted down to look at her again. 'I'm a friend of Jim's too,' she confided. 'Are you going to visit him?'

If there was home anywhere in the world it was with Young Jim. 'If I can get there. Maybe I can get a lift up to the train.'

The woman looked at her curiously. 'The train? The train line's been closed for twenty years.'

Barbara shook her head helplessly. 'Maybe I can hitch a ride then. I don't know.'

The small girl looked at her mother. The woman met her eyes, then shrugged. She seemed to come to a decision.

'There's a bus leaves from the hotel this afternoon. I don't know what time, you'll have to ask. It picks up the high school kids. You ask the driver, he'll drop you at the depot for the Sydney bus.' She glanced down at her daughter, then back at Barbara. 'Have you got any money?' Her mouth tightened. 'I didn't think so.'

She opened her handbag and took out two ten dollar notes and two fives. 'This'll get you to town and onto the bus.' She looked exasperated. 'I need to have my head read, I really do. You know where the hotel is?' She took the small girl's hand firmly, as though determined to lead her away before she found any other disreputable creatures to befriend. 'Come on, we really have to go.'

The small girl turned for one last word. 'What's your name?'

'Barbara,' said Barbara.

'Barbara.' The child tested it on her tongue. 'You'll be seeing Jim then? You say hello from me. Tell him the black cat had kittens and I'll keep him one.'

'I'll tell him,' promised Barbara. 'What's your name?'

The small girl gave one last blinding smile. 'Sara,' she recited. 'My name is Sara Dulcie Ryan.'

SEARCHING
FOR JIM

The bus poured through the tunnel of the night. There was nothing to see except the guideposts flickering through the dark and the broken edges of the highway. The other journey had been in darkness too, but there had been Young Jim warm beside her, and the smell of soap and ash and soot and metal, and the comforting clack-clacking of the train. This was faster, but so much lonelier. Finally, she slept.

She woke as the bus pulled into the depot in central Sydney. The world seemed grey. There was no fireman to hand her slabs of bread and jam, no kookaburras calling in the distance. A vending machine burped coffee into someone's cup in the waiting room. A few early cars pulled up at the traffic lights across the road.

The bus driver stared at her as she got out. He had seemed wary about letting her on the bus with her bare feet and tangled dirty hair. There was blood on her hands where a cut had opened up again — she must have torn the skin scrabbling at the boulder and not noticed. He had accepted her money in the end, nodding her to a vacant seat down the back. She thought of the money in her pocket.

Sixty cents left after the bus fare. Enough for a phone call, but not for another bus ride.

Eastcliff Private Hospital. If it was close, she'd be able to walk there. She was so hungry. How long had it been since she'd eaten Ma's thick stew? Sixty years ago ... her stomach thought it had been sixty years at least ...

She had to ask someone or find a map. Would the clerk at the desk help her? They might just throw her out, looking like this. A police car pulled up beside her as the traffic lights turned red.

For a moment she hesitated, remembering the faces at the demonstration. Then Sergeant Ryan's face erased them. She stepped onto the road without further thought and spoke through the window.

'Excuse me. Can you tell me how far it is to Eastcliff?'

The policeman was young. He stared at her, taking in the mud and the blood on her hands.

'Eastcliff? That's over past Manly.' His voice was deep, reminding her of Gully Jack. His hands were big too, but soft where Gully Jack's had been hard, and pink where his had been brown, with trimmed nails instead of cracked and dirty ones.

'Manly!' That would take hours to walk, days even.

The policeman was still staring at her. 'You live out at Eastcliff? You look like you've been in the wars. You had an accident or something?'

Barbara began to shake her head, then nodded. She *had* been in an accident.

The policeman sighed. 'Come on, hop in. I'll give you a lift out there. I'm just going off duty. I'm headed that way myself. What's your address?'

Barbara hesitated. 'Not to my home. I have to get to the hospital ... Eastcliff Private Hospital. My friend's a patient there.'

'Well, hop in if you're coming. Come on. Quick.' The lights had changed; other drivers were impatient. The policeman reached over and opened the door. 'I know where the hospital is, my granny had her veins done there. Come on, get that seat belt on, the light'll be red again in a sec.'

The seat was soft after the bus.

'What happened to you?'

Barbara repressed an urge to giggle hysterically. What would he say if she told him? Would he be angry, thinking she was having him on, or think she was a mental case?

'It's a long story. I ... just got caught up in something, that's all.'

'Something muddy by the looks.' The policeman changed gears, glanced at the blood on her arm, the dirty bare feet.

'What's your friend's name?' The voice was a shade too casual, as though checking that there really was a friend. Bare feet and ragged jumper couldn't be accounted for by an accident.

'Jim O'Reilly.'

'Jim O'Reilly?' The policeman chuckled. 'You don't mean Young Jim O'Reilly by any chance? Do you really know him?'

'You know Young Jim too?'

'Never met the bloke, but I've read about him enough. There was an article in the paper the other day. He broke his hip or something, didn't he, on that picket line? Silly old bastard, you'd think he'd be old enough to know better.' The policeman grinned. 'I wouldn't say that in front of my dad, though. The old man's his hero, always has been. Youngest-ever member of parliament back in the old days, that's what the article said. That's how he got his name, Young Jim, I reckon. He's done some good things though, don't get me wrong. Is he a friend of your parents or something?'

'He's a friend of mine,' said Barbara. She clenched her hands. What if he didn't remember her? It would be so long ago for him. What if ...

The police car ran smoothly through the suburbs.

The streets smelt weird after the smells of the valley; metal and plastic. She'd forgotten the hard, biting, smell of plastic. Noisy streets, after the quiet of the gully; cars and brakes and traffic lights. How could you get so close to a place in a few weeks? How could you become so entwined with the people?

But this world was real too. This was her world. Every minute made it clearer to her. As much as she longed for the O'Reillys and the gully, this time was hers, not then.

Somewhere deep in her soul she had known that her own time would claim her once more. This was home. If only the others were here too. Her heart seemed too big to cope with suddenly. She had to find Young Jim — she *had* to.

The police car moved smoothly up the hill towards the hospital. The policeman glanced at his watch. Of course, he'd been going off duty, he must have somewhere else he wanted to go. They pulled up outside the hospital gates.

'You sure you'll be all right? You want me to wait for you? There's a parking lot around the back.'

Barbara shook her head. It seemed too much of an effort to speak, to explain. Everything seemed concentrated on seeing Jim again. It felt like years had passed now, not just the few hours since she'd seen him last. More years than she had lived, but she could feel them all.

The policeman looked relieved. He took out a notebook and scribbled something on it, then handed her the bit of paper. 'Look, if you need me, you ring that number. Got it? I don't like leaving you, but my friend'll be waiting. She gets mad if she waits too long! You got some money on you? Here then. No, keep it, no arguing, you can send it back sometime if you want to. That's my name written down there.' She watched him drive off down the hill.

The hospital smelt clean, the sort of clean that seeps into you and won't let go. She thought for a moment that the nurse at the desk was going to order her out. But she didn't. She turned her eyes away from Barbara's dirty feet and gestured down the hall.

The mud had dried now. It felt hard, as though it was cracking and sucking all the moisture out. Her arm hurt. Her heart beat like a hammer in her chest.

Rooms with tidy beds and tidy people, too ill or too old to make a mess, under tightly stretched sheets and light, bright blankets; curtains at the windows that looked like they'd been starched; thick lino on the floor so her feet hardly made a noise. One room, two. It must be this one here.

She paused at the door. There were four beds inside. Two were empty, an old man was sleeping in another. Was it Jim? It couldn't be. Even after sixty years ...

A man was reading a magazine in the last bed. His face was bored, as though the magazine held no interest, just something for his hand to hold and his eyes to wander over. He wore striped pyjamas and bifocal glasses. His hair was brushed and faded, but not the pale colour that she'd known. This hair was grey.

The man looked up. She knew him then. It was the man she'd met at the first demonstration, who'd told her to walk around the corner.

The man stared. The magazine fell to his knees.

'Bubba,' he said.

She felt like she'd come home.

BACK WITH JIM

'Thellie rang,' said Jim.

'Thellie?'

'That was her daughter, Julie, down by the creek, and her grandkid. You remember, Sara?'

'She was Thellie's grand-daughter?'

'They were going to have lunch with her. Sara told Thellie all about you. This peculiar girl all muddy in the creek. Thellie guessed it was you as soon as she heard the name. She drove straight up to the bus depot, looking for you, but you'd just gone. Julie thought she was crazy! I've been waiting. Hoping,' said Jim.

'It's funny, isn't it?' Jim leant back against the pillows as though the shock was too heavy for his shoulders to bear. One hand trailed awkwardly across the bed. 'You reckon you've come to the end of your life, then something happens. I was just lying here thinking there was no more to my life than what they'll bring me in for tea: sloppy custard and burnt chops, or sloppy fruit and half-cooked sausages. Then you walk in, calm as a kitten in a basket, as if you'd walked around the corner.'

Barbara smiled. It seemed like years since she'd smiled, not hours.

'I did,' she said.

'I always knew you'd come back,' said Jim. His eyes were the same, still sky-blue, the colour of the sky above Poverty Gully, not the smudged city sky outside. His hands were old, swollen and wrinkled and big-knuckled, with brown splotches on the skin, but his grin was just the same.

She was sitting beside his bed. He'd made the nurse bring her a cup of tea and a plate of sandwiches, the same bossy Jim as years ago, and he'd watched her sternly while she ate them, not letting her speak until she had.

Barbara put the plate down. The world was coming into focus for the first time since she'd seen the bank crumble into the channel.

'The others didn't believe me.' Jim tried to put the magazine back on the table by his bed. He fumbled, and it slipped. Barbara picked it up for him and slipped it onto the shelf.

'Oh, they said they believed me,' Jim went on. 'They didn't want to upset me, or Thellie either for that matter. Thellie refused to believe you were dead too. She must have cried for days after you left. Every time someone came through the door she expected it to be you. As for me — well, boys that age don't think they can cry. It'd have been better for me if I had.'

'Why did everyone think I was dead?'

Barbara sipped the last of the tea. It was very strong and sweet.

'Because the flood had swept you away, of course.' Jim peered at her over his glasses. 'There were search parties looking for your body for weeks. They must've poked around every square inch of the creek, and the hills too, in case you'd managed to crawl up looking for help. Then they all looked again when the flood went down, hoping to find your body.

'I don't think Ted Ryan slept for three days, he was so upset. He organised every able-bodied man in the district.'

Jim looked out the window. 'They couldn't understand why I wasn't out there helping them. Put it down to shock, I think. But I was looking down, remember. I saw you go. One minute you were there, with your eyes shut and the next you weren't, wham bam, nothing. I hardly had time to blink, then the flood water was swirling round where you had been.

'I knew you hadn't drowned. None of the others had been watching, they hadn't seen what I had. They thought I just didn't want to face that you were dead.' He looked at her for a moment. 'That was, what — sixty years ago now. I don't suppose there's been a day since when I didn't think of you and wonder what had happened, wonder when I'd see you again. I believed I would, you know. I knew you would be somewhere in the future, waiting for me. Somewhere around the corner.' He glanced at the mud on her face, at the mud on her hands. 'I reckon it wasn't so long ago for you, was it? You've just got here.'

Barbara nodded.

'Struth, love, it must be hard for you, straight from there to here. How did you get here — to the hospital, I mean?'

'A policeman drove me here. A young one, he was nice. Jim, what happened when I left? Is everyone still there, down in the gully? Did you all move to Gully Jack's? What about the school?'

Jim nodded vaguely, as though he hadn't heard. He

seemed to be thinking. His face looked tired, older than when she had come in, as though the strain of meeting her had exhausted him. Finally he reached into the drawer beside the bed. He drew out a set of keys and handed them to her.

'What are these for?'

'The keys to my place. Go on, take them.'

'But I can't.'

'Where else are you going to stay then?'

Barbara was silent.

'You get a taxi there. They'll call you one from the front desk. You ask the sister in charge. Look, I know it's not the best staying there on your own, but it's only for a few days. With luck they'll let me out soon, and if not — well, we'll work something out. But you go home and get yourself cleaned up. Struth, Ma would say you looked like something the cat dragged in. And here,' he said, handing her some notes from his wallet, 'you get yourself some clothes too. Hell's bells, that's still Dulcie's skirt you're wearing, isn't it? I wouldn't have thought I'd remember it, but the memory's still as plain as day. Oh, and get some decent shoes. You buy some tucker, too, there won't be much that's any good in the house by now. No, don't argue!'

His eyes were the same bright blue eyes of comfort and determination. 'You just keep the home fires burning till I get back,' ordered Young Jim, 'and if you feel up to it, you come and see me in the morning. We'll tackle all your questions then.'

LOOKING
BACKWARDS

It was a lovely street — old-fashioned houses were just glimpsed through gardens, the scent of the sea beyond. The taxi pulled up by a white-painted fence.

'This is it. Number 56.'

Barbara opened the taxi door and held out the money. 'Thank you.'

The driver glanced at the house. It had an air of desertion; blank windows and shaggy grass. 'You sure this is right?'

'It's right,' said Barbara.

She opened the gate. It was metal, painted white to match the fence, but cracking now in the sunlight.

Lavender and rosemary shrubs brushed against her as she moved up the path. She remembered them from Dulcie's garden. And, what was it again? crepe myrtle — even an apple tree like Dulcie's there at the side of the house, laden with over-ripe fruit that should have been picked weeks before. Soft apples squashed into the grass all around it. The house looked like it was dozing, all alone.

Barbara turned the key in the lock and opened the door.

A gust of old air toppled through the doorway, bringing scents of floor polish, old carpets and shut-up rooms.

The house felt like a house she knew, almost, but also a stranger's house. The floors creaked as though talking to a friend. She turned the TV on to have a voice in the echoing rooms, as she wandered from room to room, looking for things that might tell her about Jim.

Photos by his bed ... two women who looked vaguely familiar; children somewhere at the beach, years ago, by the look of their swimming costumes; a kid's birthday party with a house behind. The house looked familiar, too, and then she recognised it. It was Gully Jack's house, but freshly painted, with flowers on all sides and a black and white dog — surely not the same one — up on the verandah.

Books in nearly every room. Novels in one of the spare rooms, where she'd made up the bed for herself. Books on economics, politics, philosophy, thick and dusty, in the room that must be his study, with a desk looking out into the garden. A pile of magazines and newspapers, all more than three weeks old, on the coffee table in the living room. A cup and saucer, and a plate with two stale crusts on it, unwashed by the sink. She washed them slowly, and dried them, then found where to put them away.

She found the phone in the hall. There were menus from take-away food shops that home-delivered up on the wall. She chose a pizza from the list, then rang and ordered it. She ate it sitting on the floor watching TV. It was great to eat a pizza again. She hadn't realised she'd missed them, there in the past. She hadn't realised she'd missed so many things. She took out the wooden lizard and put it on the table by the bed, so she could see it when she woke.

Jim's house was almost like a home. Almost. When Jim came back, perhaps it would be.

She went to the hospital the next day, dressed in new jeans and T-shirt and white sandals that clicked on the shiny floor. Jim was waiting for her, his face bright and expectant as she came in the door. He looked at her with approval.

'That's better. You looked like you were going to drop if you took another step yesterday. Sleep well?'

Barbara nodded. 'Sort of,' she said. 'My dreams were too bright.' She sat down on the chair by the bed. 'Jim, what happened when I left? I've got to know everything.'

Jim settled the pillows behind him more comfortably with his hand. 'I don't know where to start,' he told her. 'You have to remember it's sixty years for me, even if it's just yesterday for you.'

'Did you move down to Gully Jack's?'

Jim's grin flashed. 'Yeah, we all moved down to Gully Jack's. He told us it was your idea. Ma cried when she heard that. We didn't go for a few weeks, though. We were all out looking for you.'

Jim's face grew lively with memory. 'You should have seen Ma down at Gully Jack's. She was like a dog with two tails, couldn't work out which one to wag first. I think she spent the next month at the stove — sponge cake, apple cake, orange cake, mutton pies — if you could bake it she made it. Gully Jack even took to stopping work early just to get more time to eat.'

'Did he find the gold? The nugget?'

Jim stared at her. 'So there really was a nugget! Thellie kept saying there was, but you know what little kids are like. We thought she imagined it, or it might just have been the light shining on a bit of quartz.'

'I think it was a nugget,' said Barbara slowly. 'It was down in the mud. We were looking at it when Thellie slipped.'

Jim shook his head. 'Well, if it was there, no-one ever found it. The walls collapsed in the flood and Gully Jack didn't have the heart to repair them, not after what happened to you. He built another channel a little way down, but he didn't find much in it — a few ounces, when all was said and done. He dug another channel a few years later, and then more after that. He finally found a decent seam the year before he died, but he was so stiff with the arthritis that he couldn't do much with it.'

'When did he die?'

Jim rubbed his chin. 'Must be twenty years ago now, bit less maybe. Ma and Dad were still living in the house when he died. He left the house to them in his will, and the rest of the farm, though Dad had bought most of it from him by then. Dad started growing peaches after the war. You ever heard of gully peaches? Sweetest in Australia. They became real close, those three. Did you know Ma was the first woman on the local council? She ran against old Nicholson and beat him. You should have seen Dad and Gully Jack campaigning for her. Dad's grin was as wide as the creek when she won.' Jim smiled at the memory. 'They're all in the cemetery down in the gully. I reckon on good days Gully Jack can still hear the creek.'

Barbara was silent. Of course they couldn't be alive. She'd known it, really. How could you cry for someone dead so long ago? She felt a warm hand on hers. She looked up. Jim nodded, his face full of understanding. They sat quietly for a while.

'How about Dulcie?' Barbara asked. 'She didn't marry Gully Jack then?'

'Dulcie? She's up in town, in the hospital. The oldest resident.'

'She's still alive?'

'Too right she is. Still got all her wits about her, too. They don't make them like Dulcie any more. You should have seen her last birthday party. The whole valley must've been there and enough candles to start a bushfire.

'She's been widowed about thirty years now. She married Sergeant Ryan a few months after you left.' Jim smiled to himself. 'They had two kids. Mark, he married Thellie's daughter, Julie. You met Julie by the creek. They had a daughter, too. Jean, that was her name. You should have seen her hair in those days — heaps of red curls on her head, like snakes arguing among themselves. Her dad said his mother had hair like that.'

'It sounds like you liked her,' said Barbara.

'Yeah, I liked her,' said Jim. 'She was just like her mum, though. If there was an orphaned lamb or wombat she'd be looking after it.' He grinned. 'I married her after the war.'

Barbara stared. 'But — wasn't she much younger than you?'

'Fifteen years. It seemed a lot when we were growing up. She was, oh, she must've been about seven when I went off to war in 1940, just a kid with grubby feet and teeth all crooked where her big ones were growing in. She wrote to me all through the war. She was a good kid.

'I met Muriel, my first wife, in New Guinea. She was a nurse. Muriel died in '49. It was one of those things that hit you out of the blue. We'd both survived the war and then a car swerved around a corner, up on the footpath and hit Muriel. A couple of years later I noticed that Jean had grown up. We had three kids. They're grown up now, of course. Michael's a computer engineer overseas, Angie's still studying, and Helen, she's the oldest, is a doctor now, down at the gully. Helen and her family live in Dulcie's house at the old dairy farm, though it's all beef cattle now.'

'What about Elaine, and Joey and Harry, and Thellie?'

Jim's face grew shadowed. 'Joey died. Polio. It was bad that year. Kids don't die from polio any more but they did then.' Jim was silent for a moment

'He said he wanted a thousand sausages!'

'Well, he got those at least. Gully Jack got him all the sausages he could eat for his birthday, the one after you left. Maybe not quite a thousand ... he was nine when he died. Harry's an engineer, he'll be retiring soon. Elaine? She's still working. Elaine's like Ma. She'll work till she drops. She's a paediatrician down in Melbourne.'

'A children's doctor? But she said she never wanted to see another lot of grubby brats in her life.'

'Well, she changed her mind,' said Jim drily. 'She's got two kids of her own and her husband's a doctor as well. That's probably where my Helen got the idea from, her Aunt Elaine. I remember when she was about ten she found Elaine's plastic skeleton under the bed, the one she'd used for anatomy. She'd got half of it put together before we found her at it. She's like Elaine and she's like Dulcie, and I reckon there's a bit of Ma in her as well.'

'What about Thellie?'

'She still lives at Gully Jack's,' said Jim. 'Her boys mostly run the farm now. Mark and Julie live up in town with Sara. Funny, people still call it Gully Jack's. I suppose they always will. It's one of the biggest peach orchards in New South Wales now.

'You know, Thellie was the only one, besides me, who wouldn't accept that you were dead. All those stories you told her — she believed every one of them. She knew she'd see you again one day. Just like me. I can't wait to see her face when she meets you. You know, she's got eight grandkids now? I think Sara's the most like her of all of them, and not one of them would be alive if you hadn't saved Thellie from the flood.'

A trolley rattled somewhere down the corridor; morning tea and biscuits travelling from room to room. Jim stared out the window, as though there was something more to see than walls and gutters.

'There were good bits in those days as well as bad,' he said quietly. 'I reckon you didn't see the bad bits, not in those weeks you were with us. The hunger in the beginning, and the cold in winter, and Dad growing more and more despairing, and Ma just harder and wearier. You changed things, just by knowing it could be different.

'I reckon you were a catalyst for all of us. You were so convinced there was a world around the corner, you convinced us too. That's what we needed, someone to say another world was possible.'

'You think that's why I was able to go back?'

'I dunno,' said Jim slowly. 'Maybe it was a lot of things. All of us so desperate for another way of living; you so scared and wanting somewhere else as well. Maybe it was just all of us reaching out, vulnerable—'

'And yesterday by the creek — except it wasn't yesterday for you — I stopped wanting to stay, the terror and wanting to survive brought me back.'

'And I was desperately wishing you were somewhere else as well, somewhere safe.'

'So here I am.'

They were both silent for a minute. Another trolley wheeled past, click, click, click.

'You know, I reckon I got as good an education in that washhouse as I'd have got anywhere in Australia,' mused Jim. 'I learnt more from you, and Ma and Dad, and Dulcie and Sergeant Ryan, than I'd have learnt anywhere else. Ma showed me how to keep on going, no matter how hard things get. Dad showed me how to confront people to fight for what you think is right. I learnt how dreaming of a better world is the first step in making it happen. Learnt how much you can do if you all work together.' He shook his head. 'Maybe Gully Jack taught me how not to let your dreams take over. It was a good life we had in the valley, for all that things seemed crook at the time.'

'You sound like you miss it,' said Barbara.

'Yeah, I miss it,' said Jim. 'Not the hardship. Not the things like polio, not the '30s so much. It's the valley itself. That's what I miss.'

'Didn't you ever want to go back ...'

Jim looked out the window. 'Yeah,' he admitted slowly. 'Sometimes I feel as if the valley's a knot in my heart that won't unravel. It's tied up and won't let go. But somehow, something always kept me in the city, some cause or other that needed to be fought, and I kept thinking, maybe next year, or the one after that ...'

Jim's voice trailed away. 'Perhaps I needed you to take me back,' he said. His head slipped back against the pillow.

'I'd better go,' said Barbara. 'You're tired. I'll come back tomorrow if I may.'

Jim shook his head. 'I'll just have a nap. Didn't sleep much last night. I was so excited, that's all. You come back this afternoon,' he ordered her, the old Jim resurfacing. He met her eyes. 'You know, I used to try to go around the corner, just like you. At first I thought I could follow you, bring you back. Then I tried again, when Muriel died, and a couple of times in New Guinea, when things were tough. It never worked for me. Finally I realised I go around my corners by working for them, not by shutting my eyes.

'Then yesterday, just lying here thinking my life was over, things were as bad as they'd ever been. I reckon it was me who went around the corner yesterday, as well as you.

'It's funny — when I saw you in that demonstration I didn't recognise you. It was only when Thellie rang that I put two and two together.

'Now I've got a new life, something to live for. I reckon the two of us have got other corners to go around.' He touched his plastered hip. 'Give me a while and I'll even have this working again.' Jim grinned at her gently. 'You come this afternoon,' he said. 'I'll have a nap and be right as rain. There's something I want to show you then. All right?'

'All right.' Barbara bent over and kissed his cheek. His whiskers felt like prickly paper. 'Sleep well,' she said.

COMING HOME

The house was too empty to go to. Barbara bought a sandwich at a take-away cafe and sat by the harbour until it was time to go back to the hospital. The waves washed in and out, white hats and fat green bellies, slopping and slapping at the shore. The sun sucked up the morning's shadows, then spat them out the other side; tiny shadows that lengthened with the afternoon.

It was comfortable to be in her own time again. The loss of the O'Reillys, of Ma and Dad, was fading. She had pushed the grief back to years ago, where it belonged.

There was one other thing to do. She had been putting it off, trying to pretend it needn't be done. She had to ring her mother. There was a phone box up the hill. She took some change out of her pocket and dialled the numbers slowly ... 8, 6, 4 ...

She heard the ringing at the other end, over and over. If there was no-one home, she'd have to screw up her courage to ring again, and then the ringing stopped. She heard the money clang down.

'Hello, hello.' It was her mother's voice.

'Mum, it's me.'

'Who is it, who?'

The voice was vague, annoyed. She'd interrupted something. Another voice called in the distance. 'Who is it?'

'Will you shut up, I'm trying to find out. Hello. Hello!'

'It's me, Barbara.'

'Barbara.' She could almost see her mother trying to concentrate. 'Where are you ringing from? Is it a good foster home they've found you now?' Steve's voice said something in the background again. Her mother spoke louder to drown him out. 'We're just fine here, everthing's just fine. Another few weeks and I'll be right again. Everything's just fine.' Another interruption. 'Barbara love, I have to go. You'll ring again won't you?'

'I'll ring again,' said Barbara. She put the phone down.

It should have hurt. It always had before. It didn't now, just a faint ache like an old scar that will gradually heal. All she could feel was pity for her mother, and hope that one day she'd find her way around the corner too. Home was somewhere else now. The thought floated up and circled with the gulls. Just one more corner to turn and she'd be there.

She watched the waves and sat and thought. Back and forth, back and forth — like the waves she too had returned. Sixty years of the O'Reillys' time, but her true journey was just starting. This was the world that Ma and Dad and Elaine and Jim had helped create. A world with schools for everyone, and vaccination against polio. There were hundreds of small and large battles they'd been part of. This time she could face the corners to come without fear. They were there, Ma and Dad and Gully Jack, solid in the past behind her.

The breeze was sweet and salty off the sea as she climbed

the hill to the hospital. The nurse at the desk smiled at her now that the mud was washed off her, in a clean skirt and sandals. Barbara nodded to the old man in the first bed as she came into Jim's room.

He wasn't alone. A woman sat with him. She wore a denim skirt and a pale blue blouse. Her hair was brown and short. It should be in a ponytail — Dulcie always wore a ponytail — and the dress was wrong. It wasn't Dulcie's dress, the one with bright red roses that she'd worn to the Friday dance. It wasn't Dulcie. The face was similar, but there were differences. There was a hint of Jim, a sudden flash of Thellie ...

The woman stood up. She looked at Barbara carefully, as though there was a decision to be made.

The woman smiled — just like Ma, thought Barbara — and held out her arms.

Jim's face was calm. It was the face of a man who knows where he's been and where he's come to, although the journey has been long and not what he'd expected.

'This is Helen,' he told Barbara gently. 'She came up from the valley this morning. She's come to take us home.'

AUTHOR'S NOTE

Somewhere Around The Corner was inspired by stories of a 'susso camp' that was situated near my home. I've used the names of some of the people that lived there, such as Gully Jack and Dulcie, and some of their circumstances, like those of Mr Henderson, the headmaster who was retrenched when his school closed down. Apart from these, the characters in this book are not based in any way on any person, alive or dead.

Gully Jack's method of extracting gold is based on fact, but even though vast channels were made in the hopes of finding a fortune, very little gold was recovered. Many of the channels are still there, and so perhaps is the gold that Gully Jack dreamed of, if there was ever any to be found.

Poverty Gully was deserted at the beginning of World War II. Blackberries and thornbush now grow where the shanties stood and lyrebirds scratch where once there were hundreds of people. Most dole camps are remembered with horror. Poverty Gully was a place where people helped each other, and it is still spoken of with affection by those who knew it, or those who can recall the stories of their parents.

Araluen Valley
1994